Brooklyn Cruz©

A voyage of a million women

CRESHIE WRITES®

Dedicated to my Sistah, my friend, and my hero

Louisa "Lulu" Ramos

Thank you...

To my heavenly father! To my family, friends and Sistahs' for their support. Special shout out to my chapter by chapter readers, Monica, Tina, Shameex, Mimi, Jamelle, Devera and Velera. A very important thank you to my lovely sister Tia, she read chapter by chapter and edited every page. Thank you Tia for believing in me, even when I had doubts. I also would like to thank the musical artists that inspire my writing of this novelette, the legendary Luther Vandross and the wordsmith Eve.

"Growing Pains are wounds that heal over time but the pain changes you forever"

"Look at the Barbie doll over here, what you do hun kill somebody wit ya sexy body? I hope you taste as good as you look. I'll find out tonite." The muscular inflated assertive boyish female voices her *Chitachatter (Chitter Chatter)* followed by a small chuckle.

"Yeah she is sexy. I might have to ***shake the dice[1]*** on dis one."

"Don't let a big butt and a smile fool you." Brooklyn's "Hennessy" straight coated lips speak to the two lesbian muscular inflated assertive voices standing behind her towel, covering her unique natural beauty on the inmate shower line. Her "Hennessy" straight, complexion covers her old fashion soda bottle frame. Her clear,

---

[1] ***Shake the dice*** *is to take a gamble.*

smooth and strong complexion is just like her personality. A natural Indian beauty mole perfectly centered in the middle of her thick jet black eyebrows. Her eyebrows freely grow into a perfect arch. She never cut her hair, just weekly clipping of the tips. Her shiny jet black hair streams down her back and passes over the towel down a little below her butt to her mid thigh. Brooklyn agitated the two lesbians with a wink delivered from her right eye.

"You talk tough but we'll see how tough you really are once you drop the towel."

"No, we shall see now!" Brooklyn's words spilled from her "Hennessy" straight coated lips as she turns her body to face the two lesbian muscular inflated assertive voices.

Before the muscular lesbians could respond Brooklyn had stabbed one in the eye with her government issued toothbrush. Brooklyn had one on the knees holding her bloody punctured right eye. The uninjured lesbian swings a punch at Brooklyn's face. Brooklyn dodges the swing but felt the wind of it. Brooklyn positions herself behind the uninjured muscular inflated assertive lesbian and jumps on her back. Brooklyn crosses her legs around the body of the uninjured one and wraps her long jet black hair around her neck like a lasso. Brooklyn tightens her grip around the lesbian's body and continues to strangle her with her hair. It took three female correctional officers to get the uninjured woman from under Brooklyn's hold.

"1-3-R-2-6-2-8" Brooklyn's "Hennessy" straight coated lips recite her inmate numbers to the correctional officer. The intriguing state issued green slacks and short sleeved button down shirt covered her hour glass frame.

"Lock down!" the correctional officer shouts to his co-worker in the plastic bubble office towering above him.

Brooklyn returns to her prison cell. Her mind wanders to the beginning... overseas on July 17th 1980 the day her life sailed into a completely different direction.

*"I woke up early like I did every other morning. I went to the chicken coop to get eggs for breakfast. I fed the chickens before I returned to the house. My little 8 year old body carried a **guanabana**[2]. I fried eggs and plantains. I cut the guanabana open to its custard like white insides. I had to pick out the thousand and one inedible seeds. I made* **champola de guanabana**[3]. *Today is picture*

---

[2] **Guanabana** *is a ten pound green thorny fruit grown in the Dominican Republic.*

[3] **champola de guanabana** *is a Dominican delicious drink*

day. I was the face of Nova fruita. Nova fruita is a generation owned business that started 100's of years ago but is currently in my mother's possession. In DR you either export fruits, coffee, women or drugs. My mother's family tree rooted from ***carambola***[4] export. I woke up my mother and father to breakfast in bed. While they enjoyed their meal I bathed and got dressed to make rounds with my father, as I did every day. I loved the horseback ride with my arms wrapped around my father's heroic waist. Our 1st stop is at one of Papi's coffee bean farms. My two older brothers from a different woman ran this farm. Bryan and Ryan were 19 and 20 years old at this time. Both of them were always brotherly to me. Papi's scolds them every day because the farm felt like a play more than work. There were many coffee plants grown to man's size man's size ripeness. The red berries needed

---

made with guanabana pulp, milk and sugar.

[4] ***Carambola*** is a Dominican Republic grown fruit. The entire frit is edible with a mix taste of an apple, pear and orange.

to be removed from the branches. Then after the berries are removed they have to be fermented, washed and dried. It takes 9 months for a coffee plant to be ready for harvest. In the 9 months Papi had set up export buyers. The boys were accused of delaying Papi's money. The next stop is the stop I wish we didn't have to make. It's Papi's **chia**[5] Maria's house, where my half-sister Mercedes lived. Mercedes is 3 years older than me. There was no sisterly love between us. Mercedes hated me as much as I hated her. One day she told me to my face that one day Papi would be all hers and when that day came, I would never see him again. So, on every visit I broke one of her toys, tore her dress, or just pulled her hair until she cried. Today we made an extra stop. This stop was rare and it was the stop I hated the most. We went to Papi's sister's house, Titi Rosa. Titi Rosa gives Papi an ear full. Titi Rosa felt like since Papi made good money off all 3 coffee bean farms, he could

---

[5] **Chia** translates to mistress from Spanish to English..

afford to pay her more. She was tired of doing all the work while he gained the dollar benefit. Brooklyn's ***chitachatter.***[6]

"Lights out!" the correctional officer shouts again to his co-worker in the plastic bubble office towering above him as he walks pass Brooklyn's gray four wall home.

---

[6] ***Chitachatter [Chitter Chatter]*** *is the ultimate form free of expression. It's things swimming around in your head but never floats anywhere. It can be bias chaotic conversations between yourself. It might be a song playing. A melody you haven't heard in years. Lyrics, mentally returns you to a day the sounds represents. Perhaps, a persisting replaying tunes ringing between your ears. The repetition of musical buzzing, have you murmuring the jingle. It happens to everyone. Stop twisting up your face; it's one hundred percent true. If anyone says otherwise, they're lying. How many times have you heard people say "Something was telling me..." ,"I got this song in my head and I just can't get it out." or been asked to guess the name of a song off of a humming clue. It's the biosphere where words can't be characterized. Words can't be accused of being politically incorrect by passing the need to bandage up any battered feelings. Facts, hearsay and opinions have a tendency to bruise. Chitachatter transpires inside your head and is assumed to stay there.*

"*Titi Rosa spotted the* **sangre**[7] *on my shorts. When I looked down the sangre was rolling down my legs. Titi Rosa called* **Curandera**[8] *right over. Titi Rosa and Papi argued about the sangre. I had no idea what was going on. But once* **Curandera** *arrived I kinda figured out what had happen to me. I was 8 yrs. old and had just entered into womanhood by having my 1st period. Papi said it was unsafe to take me back home by way of horseback riding. I had to spend the next 5 days at Titi Rosa's house. Titi Rosa had me working on the coffee bean farm, cooking and cleaning her whole one story 3 bedroom house. Titi Rosa didn't have a husband because she couldn't have kids. This fact about Titi Rosa's life made her bitter and mean. I think she didn't have kids 'cus she just didn't like them. I knew she didn't like me. So I did what I was told and would disappear quickly. Thanks to Curandera's advice Titi Rosa was forbidden to feed me for the 5 day*

---

[7] **Sangre** *translates to blood.*

[8] **Curandera** *translates to a female healer.*

stay. I was more than happy and hungry to return home. Papi came and picked me up from Titi Rosa's house and dropped me off at home along with a message from Curandera. Curandera claims the sangre has cursed me. My mother ate up the belief in Curandera's words. Within seconds of being home I could feel my mother's heart warmth turn cold. By the third visit of the sangre my body started to change. The change was painful. The budding of breast was like bee stings on my chest, burning with red hot sensation. I would hold ice cubes on my chest to cool down the growing pains. These breast growing pains lasted for 10 months but when one pain stopped another pain begun. I became the fault of wrongs in my mother's house. First, the coffee beans plants had dried up. My mother summed up matters to be the beginning of the curse that Curandera predicted. With the coffee beans plants dried, Papi found another farm to groom into his business. Papi's occasional vacations home became less and less frequent. And the father-daughter relationship we once shared was fading. In Papi's eyes there were looks that don't just ease by you. Papi had the same look Kelbe, the old man that sells fruit on the road has when he offers me free fruit. That lusty look that makes me feel dirty. One day when Curandera came to my mother's house I hid to listen. My ears could have burned off from the words flying from this old woman's mouth. She said I had the gift of beauty and the curse of death. The curse treatment was to be married and bring life into the world. "But I predict by that time she would have taken so much from so many" was her fucked up reading. My mother asked about Papi. According to Curandera, Papi has dreams of being in the arms of another woman. The dreams are what was keeping him from returning home permanently. That bitch Curandera would tell my mother fucked up "temporary" cures to my curse. My mother had washed my body from head to toe with streaming hot water and a scrub brush. My father came running to my aid. This was the only time Papi found his way home after being lost for two weeks to three weeks at a time. Thanks to Curandera's twisted advice my skin was sore and ripped; sensitive to a look. I would hide my period to avoid the brutal wicked cleanse. Then I would be beaten and accused of being fondled by a boy. I selected the brutal wicked cleanse with egg yolk, pig's guts and chicken blood over the beating with a hair brush. From the brutal wicked cleanse I always had a trail of flies following me. When the brutal wicked cleanse stopped wrenching Papi back into my mother's arms, depression had taken over her being. When Papi did come around his attention was focused on me. He completely ignored my mother. As his visits faded to just not showing up, his money disappeared also. My mother was living off of the crumbs for the family business. I could never understand the sacrificial love emotion. How could my mother love someone more than she loved herself? How could she just give up on life? She laid in the bed for weeks *without eating or bathing like she was just waiting on death. How could she just forget I was still here? Chyenne and Tay also suffered from this sacrificial love for a man. I couldn't wrap my mind around it when my mother was under the influence of the sacrificial love and still didn't get it when Chyenne and Tay was sick from the same disease. My mother would have spontaneous insane breakthroughs like killing all the chickens in the coop and washing the walls of the house and me with the chicken's blood. On my tenth birthday I woke up and walked into the living room to find my mother with a rope tied to a curtain rod in the threshold between the kitchen and the living room. The other end of the rope was around my mother's neck as she stood on a chair. I looked straight into her eyes. There was no life in her eyes. No love, no spirit; just a shell of a human. As much as I didn't want her to suffer I wanted her to be free from the ailment of a weak heart. My Impetuous nature kicked the chair from under her. Later* *in life a Psychiatrist asked me how did I feel about the death of my mother and I'll tell y'all like I told her, my mother was a prisoner of a **locked heart** [9]and I freed her from the pain that had damaged her mentally. She would've never healed."*

***

"I'm not going no fucking where! If she's in jail it's for a good reason and it's about time. She should've been locked up for killing Papi." Edwin speaks through his horrendous brandy coated lips.

"Did you forget we are talking about our mother? I don't give a fuck what she did I'm going to get her. Either you come or not but I'm going and I'm taking money out of our bank account with me." Dino declares his love and

---

[9] **Locked heart** *is Sistah talk for being locked up in all types of wrong love but the heart still gripping on to what will never be.*

dedication for his mother to his brothers.

"Have you completely lost ya fucking mind? You are going to give her more of Papi's money? That bank account belongs to all four of us. We all have to agree before you just take money out. Shit, she's a thug she'll be fine. She made it through 30 days already." Pedro announces his protest against Dino's decision.

"She did 30 days in the hole for choking a chick up in there with her hair. She is one tough cookie but once she is in general population I don't think she'll be safe. We gotta get her outta there." Miguel speaks his concern for his mother.

"That's two against two. Which one of you gonna break the tie? 'Cus I'm going to get her out."

"She killed Papi! How could you two be so gung-ho about getting her free? She is a menace on these streets. She knocked Titi Joanny out, tasered Lewis, shot Roc and everybody believes she killed the guy from L.A. The streets are safe with her off them. I say fuck her! And that's just for Papi." Pedro states his final decision.

"Both of you kill me with this Papi shit. Edwin do you remember how Papi put a cigarette out on ya chest? Pedro you forgot how Papi fucked Amanda, on your bed in your face?" Miguel had to dig into his brothers' terrorized childhood memories of their father to make them part with the money.

Amanda is Pedro's first love and the mother of his questionable son.

***

"I'm going to tell you again. Any evidence you find will not be helpful to Brooklyn's case because of your connection to her. We all want to help her because we all know her. That's why I gave the case to another precinct. Don't lose ya job over this. You should focus on your wife. She really needs you." Captain Woodard scolds Omar, Tay's brother in-law, on his rebellious actions.

***

"We gonna have to split up. I'm going to the hospital to check up on Tay. And you go to the court to find out if they gonna let Brooklyn out. Dino said he gonna meet you there with some money, just in case the judge let her out on bail" Rhonda breaks down the plan with Sammy.

***

"After my mother's death I lived in the house a whole 6 months before Enrique found mother's dead body in the cellar. Enrique was then and still is the one who keeps the Nova fruita business alive and produces money. Papi's mother's sister Silvia came to live and care for me. She showered me with the love my mother had lost. Silvia became the mother I once had. I loved Silvia like she was my mother. After a year of living and being a 10 year old girl Silvia got sick out of nowhere. I thought I had escaped the curse but instead the curse had caught up to me. I begged Papi to move me to my brothers' house. As much as I wanted to stay by Silvia's side I didn't want her to die. It killed me to leave the love behind but I had to. After 3 months of living with my brothers, Silvia was cured. Living with Bryan and Ryan was informative. I learned why Papi ran away from my mother. It was because of my body. Papi was sexually tempted by my beauty and he didn't want to do to me what his father did to Titi Rosa. Titi Rosa's beauty had *persuaded her father to rape her at the age of 10 years old. The merciless rape had damaged Titi Rosa's child bearing organs. My brothers taught me how to scam, shoot a gun and fight. They would take me out to the local clubs on the weekends. While they hoax females on to the dance floor I would examine the female's property for money or anything of value. At the end of the night we would split the winnings down three ways. Jorge, the owner of one of the clubs knew exactly what we were doing but still let us in because he had those eyes that "don't just ease by you", on me. Jorge even gave me a job at the club. I was the cashier. Bryan and Ryan had me switching fake money for real money out the cash register. After 6 months Jorge got wise to the swip and swap. One morning after my brothers dropped me off to work, Jorge asked me to grab some bottles of liquor from the storage room. I was edgy about the whole thing. I knew Jorge used the storage room as his personal sexual toilet. Jorge would promise young girls the world* and have a group of guys have their way with them for a fee. The poor young girls never saw a penny from the money he made off of them. He lingered behind me. Before I could blink my eyes, Jorge was breathing down my neck. He was whispering his knowledge of the money swap and how I could go to jail. But he was willing to work something out. I heard the zipper on his pants unzip. His breathing intensified. He turned me around. His voice had changed. His tone no longer had the charm ring in his voice; the sound was more demonic than anything. He demanded I remove my clothes slowly. He took a seat next to a large light stand five feet tall. His stiff manhood in his hand as his eyes drunk up my early developed breast and swollen butt. Bryan and Ryan had a gut reaction to turn the car around and go back to the club. When they didn't find me at the front desk where I belonged, they burst through the storage room door with fire in their eyes. They couldn't believe Jorge would try to pin me up *in the storage room and make me pay with my body. My brothers had arrived just in time, I was already naked. Bryan and Ryan beat Jorge to bloody eyes, a toothless mouth and broken bones. The only thing that came from working at the club was meeting Carlito. Carlito was a frequent visitor at Jorge's spot. We had shared eyes never words."*

"A work in progress to be free of the stress. A work in progress to be forever blessed. A work in progress to have more than less of a mess I call a life."

As Brooklyn's eyes ogles the male with "Hennessy" straight complexion covering his ripened feeble firm. She inhales the brave memories of a man who stood as a hero in her youthful eyes. She exhales the reality of the man. The man sits on the armless visitor's chair. Brooklyn's vision of his cowardly beings makes the man slump in the chair. His spineless pathetic body sits awaiting Brooklyn's voice. A sound he hasn't heard in eighteen years.

"My little flower, your beauty dances in my eyes is sweeter than in my memory." The "Hennessy" straight coated man with the slumped ripened feeble firm speaks. His stamina against the silence weakened his patience.

"Look into my eyes and I need you to look deep. Tell me what do you see? Do you see my beauty? Do I look complete? Can you see pass my beauty and see your daughter? Well, use your vision to see the real me. Know me for what I am. Know me of what you and my mother made me to be and then come back to me. And come prepare to answer the same questions. I just hope for the sake of your life I'm still in this hell when you come back."

Brooklyn stands up from behind the round plastic table sitting between her and her father. She holds her head up to the correctional officer signaling she was done with the visit or more like she was done with the visitor. The correctional officer obeys Brooklyn's wishes and walks over to escort her out of the visiting area.

"Who the fuck do he think he is, Casanova? Come up in the jail with his sweet voice. I haven't seen him since he signed me over to Carlito, when I was 12 years old. Its times like these that I thank my mother for beating and cleansing me of emotion. Looking in my father eyes I felt nothing. Looking into my father's eyes I still see the ease by you glare. Does he dare stare or care to see a dead little girl. Can he see the dead little girl who waited for her hero to save her from Curandera's words? Curandera's words had cursed me. When I look in the mirror I can see the dead little girl. She is down. She cries. She is depressed. And just like me she wants to be complete but our desire is in different ways. Life is difficult but nobody promised sunshine all the time. But I was never prepared for it to rain pain every day, guaranteed. Harlem's bright lights have opened my eyes to see that it isn't impossible to have joy in the heart. I finally open my eyes to see I'm just like the dead little girl we both share the struggle, beauty always

looking face to face with trouble. I speak to her. "I'm with you.", "I feel you.", "I know you." "I'm just like you I feel your pain, we are one in the same." I'm a work in progress and I know it but does the dead little girl know it?" Brooklyn's chitachatter.

"1-3-R-2-6-2-8" Brooklyn's "Hennessy" straight coated lips recite her inmate numbers to the correctional officer.

She has changed back into her intriguing state issued green slacks and short sleeved button down shirt covering her hour glass frame from the gray visitor's jumpsuit. Brooklyn returns to her prison state of mind, housed by gray four walls she calls home. She was grateful to be released from her thirty day lockdown but the visitor was a waste of her time. Brooklyn lays on a narrow top bunk bed. Her mind has her eyes looking into the past as she stares at the prison badly painted gray ceiling.

Bryan and Ryan became DR professionals; heavy weight boxers after they were noticed for their hand technique displayed on Jorge. José Louié owns a shady boxing gym. He immediately offered Bryan and Ryan a chance of a lifetime. They trained for 3 months at night. Their blooming boxing career was a secret to Papi. They worked on the coffee farm by day and when the sunset they were at José Louié's boxing gym. I would tag along after Jorge, I was never left alone. Where ever my brothers went, I went. Carlito was also trained at the gym. My beauty had captured Carlito's eyes from the 1st time they caught sight. I always sat on the side while Bryan and Ryan trained and had practiced rounds in the ring. Carlito was the son of a heavy champion who won a ticket to the States to fight against American boxers. Carlito's father had forced him into his footsteps. Carlito was an average fighter. His vigor came from his DR street knowledge. Carlito was different from every man who locked eyes with my beauty. I know Carlito wanted my beauty just like every other man but he detained his eye's desires. I was completely attracted to his self-control. My gut flutters allowed him to talk to me. I had fell into Carlito's calm smooth brown butterscotch skin and his alluring bedroom lightly toast brown eyes. His 6 foot 2 inches of mass muscle was dancing in my eyes. My beauty needed a protector. I know I couldn't live with my brothers for too long. The curse would catch up to me. Carlito and I had been talking to each other in the gym for weeks. We even sat together at the arena when Bryan and Ryan had their first, second and third paid fights. Each fight won was a 10 thousand dollar gain to Bryan and Ryan. With the extra money they hired Esteban to tend to the coffee plants; leaving their days free. They took the time to show me the joy of being an 11 year old kid. They took me to beaches, carnivals, and to the many different fiestas Carlito was invited to; every outing at my request. Carlito and I grew closer. He wanted to take our friendly relationship a step further by taking me out, just the two of us. My brothers laughed in his face but he kept trying. I finally cracked my brothers by asking them myself. They allowed us to eat in the restaurant alone while they waited outside in their ford pickup truck. Carlito was a perfect gentleman on the date. He was holding doors, pulling out chairs, he even cleaned my mouth. He was mesmerized by my beauty but not in the ease by you creepy way. I loved the attention. I begged my brothers to allow Carlito to take me back home by way of horse instead of horse's power. Riding on the back of the horse with the night wind in my hair as the horse 4 legs danced under the moon light rain. I closed my eyes and squeezed Carlito's waist. My closed eyes saw Sunday dinner at my parent's house; back when I was curse free and innocent. Papi would hold me up high so I could dance with him and my mother. My mother's eyes stress free, joy in her voice and love in her touch. My mother would get tired of dancing and sit down. Then I would have Papi all to myself. I would stand on top of his long feet as he held my hands and we would dance the night away. I could see the love in his eyes and feel the care in his touch, and when Papi got tired I would dance solo. My father's 4 sisters Titi Rosa, Maria, Yolka and Yania would cheer me on. My great and grandparents were also in attendance, it was a family tradition. I would spin around until I fell asleep and Papi would carry me to my room. When I woke up that Monday morning Papi had left a dollar under my pillow for me. That dollar meant more than it was worth. I used to dream I was dancing with Papi to a never ending song. I wish to dance with Papi again. But when Papi moved out, the Sunday dinner followed him. I fell in love with the feeling Carlito stirred in my memory. Riding with Carlito reminded me of the day my mother would brush my hair as she sang "sweet daughter of mine" in Spanish. Riding with Carlito felt like the day when I would make rounds with Papi in the early mornings. Riding with Carlito on the horse felt new but was very familiar to my heart. We were at my brothers' house but talked under the moonlight, laid out on the grass; speaking our daydreams. I know Carlito was 21 and I was 11 but we connected in a way I never had with anyone else. I was living no more sad days or minutes. I would follow Carlito to the moon. It felt amazing to be loved again. As soon as Carlito revealed his curse about having millions awaiting him in the States but had to be married to get the money, which were his father wishes. His father didn't want Carlito to waste the money he literally fought for. His father's thinking was that with a wife and family money had a different value and Carlito would realize it. Carlito's talk of his curse called mine to light. Ryan was knocked unconscious in a boxing match and was in a coma. I had to get away fast. I loved my brother and I didn't want my curse to kill him. I ran directly to Carlito's arms. I accepted his marriage proposal and made it happen the very next day. Two days later

*Ryan woke up asking for **carambola** [10]after being out for 4 days. Papi had to show up to sign me over to Carlito. Papi's eyes sparkled with those same "ease by you" stares. His envious glares at Carlito were laughed at. The beginning with Carlito was sweet. I had no clue things would turn sour."*

***

"How much are you charging for taking the case?" Edwin's aggressive tone question shot out his butterscotch lips.

Edwin inherited Carlito's body builder frame. He intimated Marquez Ortiz, attorney at law just like Carlito did. Edwin sat across from Marquez on the opposite side of his oak wood desk.

"It's normally 25 thousand for retaining my services, and there are recurring fees. The Recurring fees

---

[10] **Carambola** *is a Dominican Republic grown fruit. The entire frit is edible with a mix taste of an apple, pear and orange.*

consists of documentation recovery and court appearances. Usually at the end of everything the bill is about 45 and we're not even talking trial" Marquez explains to Edwin and Marisol. Marisol is Edwin's wife.

Marisol sat in silence, disbelief held her tongue. She was amazed that Edwin had put up their home to help his mother. A mother she has never met or heard him speak of. In their five years of marriage Edwin has avoided any talk of his family besides his father and brothers. Marisol never questioned it. She had sat in the company of all five men and they never let their words trip them into mentioning her. This was all new to her. The office on Grand Concourse and One hundred sixty first street was gloomy. The sun's ray shooting through the window had no effect on the dull ora clouding the air. Marisol sat with tight lips and her legs tightly cross. She felt unsafe, like she was sitting on a Spanish mafia movie set.

"Sounds like you're being paid the 25 and nothing else, you have a problem with that?" Edwin questions Marquez.

Edwin's eyes stared into Marquez's face with Carlito's dark, intimidating eyes. The sight in Edwin's eyes frightened Marquez. Any deal Edwin put on the table was a deal. The look of death was a warning and Marquez was listening. Edwin as a young boy had seen Carlito hit Marquez so hard that his skin busted open. But before Carlito delivered a death hit there was a certain look in his eyes. The look was cold, deadly and scary. Edwin had mastered the look of death.

"No, no, no problem at all. I'm just surprised you're doing all this for Brooklyn. Do your brothers know about this?"

"My brothers will NEVER, EVER know about this! Do you understand? And what I do for my mother is my business."

Edwin's words were strong and delivered a message but the look in his eyes told a different story. Edwin's eyes stared into the pit of Marquez's soul and saw him as the snake weasel, Carlito reported him to be. Dino's words earlier in the day reminded Edwin of Carlito's hurtful ways. Edwin's mind also retold events of brutal attacks on his mother from Carlito's boxer built hands. Edwin's memories felt for his mother and was willing to help her with no cost. Edwin's biggest worry was Pedro finding out about it.

***

"Papi, did Amanda give herself to you or did you take it?" Pedro questions Carlito, his words trembled with fear.

"When you question a man where his dick has been, you are asking for a fight." Carlito's words were equivalent to a bell ringing in a boxing match.

"Papi, I just want to know if my son is mine or yours."
Pedro talks to his father not as his son but as a man. Before Pedro could blink his eyes, Carlito's fist was introduced to his chest, ribs and face.

Haunting Pedro's sleep is the beat down from Carlito's boxer fists. Pedro's mind was conflicted with the question of paternity of his son. He had finally mustard up enough strength to confront his father before Carlito's death. Pedro's acclaimed son was already a year old. Carlito answered Pedro's question with his fist to his face, ribs and heart. Pedro could easily get a paternity test done but he was getting a twisted pleasure by torturing Amanda and Carlito with the question.

"Pedro, wake up!" Chyna shouted to wake Pedro from his sleep.

Pedro was throwing punches in his sleep again. Chyna was hit in her head. After she was brutally awakened she decided that Pedro's time at her apartment was up.

"What time is it?" Pedro question's Chyna with fiery in his voice.
"It's time for you to leave, I'm sure your wife is looking for you." Chyna's words boiled from within.

"One day you'll be somebody's wife."

"Nope, I like being the mistress; it's twice the pleasure minus the headaches." She assured as she showed him the door.

Pedro left Chyna's apartment after a night of heavy cocaine usage and rough sex. The fun time at Chyna's apartment was to suppress his pain of the encounter with Carlito a year ago. But the ruthless beating from Carlito continues to haunt all his dreams. The worst part of if it all is Pedro still doesn't know the truth. Pedro's mind wonders if Amanda was really raped by Carlito like she claims or did she willingly give herself to him. His mind often trips over the possibility that his son may in fact be his brother. As much as he mercilessly beats Amanda, the truth would never come out. Pedro drove his midnight blue 2010 Land Rover from Washington heights to New Brunswick, New Jersey. In Jersey is the house that is shared property between himself and his brothers. Property inherited from Carlito's death. The two story gated mini mansion was once lived in by their father.

"Yo, bro where have you been Amanda called here a 1000 times. Ya son smashed his hand in something and had to get 3 stitches between his index finger and thumb. Where is ya phone at? What's wrong with you?" Miguel greets his brother at the front door with information and questions.

Pedro has been unreachable since Friday afternoon until now. It is three o'clock on a Sunday afternoon.

"Nothing's wrong with me, but the lil nicca ight, right?" Pedro nonchalantly attitude rings in his words. His hardheartedness was a gene straight from Carlito.

"That isn't the point. You're supposed to be there for your son. Raise him the ways we wasn't." Dino adds his words to the conversation.

"Who's here?" Pedro questions the sounds he hears coming from deep inside the house.

"That cocaine gotcha paranoid, ya looking just like Papi." Miguel delivers his insult with a short chuckle.

"Fuck you! Who's here? I know ya'll hear dat?" Pedro questions as his jittery eyes look around.

"Benny, Calvin and Polo are here, calm down bro, last night we turned up at a party in the village. Last night was epic." Dino confesses.

"I have told you young boys to be careful playing down in those neck of the woods. End up wit a chick wit a dick." Pedro jokes.

Miguel has already turned his attention back to his laptop. He was putting the finishing touches on last night's filming.

"Done!" Miguel announces.

"Yo bros, it's done." Dino is calling out to Benny, Calvin and Polo, to see the finished film.

They all stand around Miguel watching.

"Excellent job Miguel, you made them look like pros." Calvin jokes.

"Oh, so you are a pro?" Benny questions.

"Yes, indeed look at the camera. I had plenty of practice; this is like our 20th movie." Calvin replies.

"But you always do the same one leg up, the dougie and then smile at the camera. It looks staged." Polo reveals.

"That's my signature move, don't hate cus you aint got one." Calvin replies as he snickers.

"You guys ready? We gotta roll." Dino looks at his watch.

"Where are y'all heading to?"

"Benny has a semi-final game, and he better win cus I have already taken bets on the championship game. Me and Polo are gonna check up on our moms. Dino is gonna go check Lewis."

Tay's children are taking shifts to care for her. Calvin has the afternoon shift. Polo is going to the hospital to see his mother Chyenne. Dino is going to have a discussion with Lewis regarding Harlem's future.

***

"I think it's the perfect time to file for full custody. How many times will Brooklyn find herself in a similar situation? It's not fair to Harlem. A child needs a stable home. Can you honestly say Brooklyn will be able to provide that to her for the next 14 years?" Lewis speaks across the desk.

"Samantha, you know Brooklyn better than we do, and you know she is a wild card. Her actions are unpredictable and a 4 year old can't live under those conditions. Some might even classify it as child abuse." Vanessa, Lewis's wife, sugar coats her blatant disrespect.

"That's a bitch ass nicca move to kick her while she's down? I got one better I would love to see you say all that to my mother's face and then count how many teeth you have left. The nerve of these two, who do they think they are?" Dino replies with distaste in Lewis's suggestions.

"Dino please relax." Sammy's court room manner is in the tone of her words.

"Please calm down grown folks are talking." Lewis stabs at Dino.

"Lewis, as Brooklyn's attorney and Sistah I can't discuss her open case with you but I can ask are you really winning if there's nobody to fight? And Vanessa this fight has nothing to do with you. I strongly suggest you just watch from the sideline. I think the best thing, no the ADULT thing for us to do is to just wait until Brooklyn is out to make her own moves." Sammy's words are set in the air to defuse the brewing situation.

"Carlito's way of love and life creates the immortality of being his wife"

"*Who is this bitch? I really hope this bitch aint here to bare bad news. I definitely could have stood in my cell. I'm dealing with more than one care to endure. What could she possibly want, from me?*" Brooklyn's chitachatter interrogates in her head.

"I know you are wondering why I am here. But I have no one else to turn to. I don't want nothing more but an ear to listen to me."

"I'm all ears." Brooklyn sits up straight and speaks to the pale fragile woman with worn eyes.

Brooklyn's hardened demeanor softens after staring at the woman's eyes. The all cried out look is a familiar look to Brooklyn's eyes. She also has been broken from inside-out and her eyes told the same tale the woman's eyes were speaking to Brooklyn's heart.

"First and foremost I want to thank you for saving me that night. I want you to know the whole story. I married your son Pedro, 3 years ago and your husband brutally raped me... a year after the wedding."

The woman takes a pause between the stream of tears and snot running down her face. Her emotions spontaneously get caught in her throat. Her voice trips over her raw emotions willingly being exposed. The words she speaks have never fell into air.

"I have told your son 100 times that I was... raped... but he doesn't believe me...and to make matters even worst... Pedro completely ignores my 1 year old son...he walks by my son like a total stranger..."

The woman's pain in her words were just as visible to Brooklyn like the black and blue mark on the inside of the woman's forearm. The woman pulls out her handkerchief to soak up her emotional bruises. Brooklyn's scabs of the past from the cuts to her heart were one in the same as the woman's fresh sores.

"I want to thank you...for saving me...I went to Carlito's store...to try to get him...to admit...he raped me...I had the...recorder...in my pocket...but I never pressed record...my hands wouldn't stop shaking..."

"Why did you go there alone? Carlito is a lot to handle for many men. For women forget about it."

Brooklyn and the woman are reminiscing on their unofficial introduction. Brooklyn had gained knowledge that from the day Carlito married her he was receiving ***Nova fruit's*** [11] profit. Before Carlito was benefitting from *Nova fruita's*, Brooklyn's father was collecting the revenue. Brooklyn had her heart set on demanding what was rightfully hers. Brooklyn was trained on how to deal with Carlito. Brooklyn walked right into Carlito's ***bodega*** [12]. She disregarded the sixteen year old cashier's shouts to not go any further and continued walking towards the back office like the teenager wasn't even there. The teenage girl called out to Brooklyn's back. Brooklyn's mind was set

---

[11] ***Nova fruita's*** is Brooklyn's family Dominican Republic base fruit export business.

[12] ***Bodega*** translates to grocery store.

and her ears were closed. Brooklyn walked in on Carlito. Carlito had the back of his muscular right forearm to the woman's throat. He had her pinned to the wall and his hand was crawling around inside her shirt. Brooklyn presence stole his attention from the woman. He stood staring at Brooklyn like his eyes were playing tricks on him. The woman scurried to freedom with her body intact but her emotions were a wreck.

"Please forgive me if I offend you but what happened after I left?" The woman's inquiry flows with concern but the look in her eyes questions if Brooklyn killed Carlito? He was found dead the next morning in his car, one shot to the back of his head.

Brooklyn sums up the visits with pleasantries and returned to her cell. Brooklyn had to be subjected to being stripped of her pride while being naked. Brooklyn lies on her thin twin size mattress. Her eyes stare up at the ceiling of cracked paint but her chitchatter takes her vision to the past.

"I had to wait 3 months for my 12th birthday before me and Carlito could be an official married couple. Those 3 months I boiled with anticipation of how life was going to be, new home, a husband and close to being curse free. My brothers spent the 3 months trying to convince me that I had "other choices". That fucking bitch had twisted my mother's mind and mine at the same time. I believed if I stayed I would I have lost one or both of my brothers. At that point in my life I was a believer and I wasn't gambling with my brothers' lives and Carlito wasn't bad at all. He was a perfect gentleman to my 11 year and 9 month old eyes. I wanted to be with him as much as he wanted to be with me. Finally, the wait was over and I was

dropped off at the front steps of Carlito's house. I hugged and kissed my brothers with joy in my voice and love in my heart. They would never admit it but they were happy for me. I was happy for me. Carlito gave me a tour of the newly purchased house with a wonderful garden in the backyard and field in the front. Carlito announced that he would handle the front and I would handle the back. Anything he pitched out his mouth I caught. We made dinner together. He tried to pull the age card. But I was cooking since I was 8. I was in the kitchen showing off with knots in my stomach the whole time. After dinner, Carlito bathed me. My heart had completely stopped beating a number of times in my youthful age I had only been completely naked in front of my parents and Jorge by force. His manly hands on my young tender skin sparked the jitters in my bones. I stop breathing when his hand caressed my budding breast and between my legs. He led me by the hand into a room of candle lights. Carlito disappeared for a *good 15 minutes. I was just standing there looking around. I wondered where he could've gone. Just when I was about to reach for the bedroom door knob, Carlito whisked the door open and he was back in the room. He declared his plan to begin with me and end with the young girl sitting on the living room couch. I stood in a towel but I felt bare. He walked up to my developed frame but undeveloped mind and planted his lips on top of mine. He made his tongue swim inside my mouth. My heart continued to pound. He freed my hand from holding up the towel. He laid me on the king size bed. My heart was beating so fast I could hear it clearly in my ears. His lips and tongue explored my flesh and youth. His lips latched on to my nipple. He licked, nibbled and sucked my nipples until they were sensitive to air for the next week. His tongue trailed down toward between my legs. My inexperienced legs naturally locked at the knees. As his hands analyzed every inch of my youthful skin above the waist. He* eyeballed my beauty. It was like he was in a trance being led by the "spell". I confessed on the spot that I had not gone this far with any boy ever and I wasn't willing to go that far that night. Carlito followed his plan and processed to the teenage girl in the living room. Carlito stripped and my eyes fell out of my head. I had never seen a boy or man's penis. The teenager received him with open legs. He packed the girl with all of himself. While Carlito pounded into the girl his eyes were locked on me. It was like he wished the girl receiving the brutal stabbing was me. In a twisted way Carlito's sexual acts with the teenage girl was a term of endearment. In his warped mind he was persevering my innocence by exposing my eyes to sex and not my body. After Carlito finished with her, he showed her the door. He showered. I just sat still. The images of the night flipped in random order in my mind. Carlito lead me from my statue state to the bedroom. He cuddled me in his arms the whole night. Tears rolled down my cheeks, his embrace had the scent of my mother. She would hold me and sing her angelic Dominican voice in my ear until I fell asleep. As Carlito held me I could hear my mother's singing in the air. His penis pressed up against my ass was new but welcomed. The next morning I felt alive. I hadn't slept through the night since I was 8 years old. The curse haunted my dreams. I was up before Carlito. I couldn't wait to show off my cooking skills. I made ***huevos criollos Dominicanos***[13] y ***mangu***[14]. I prepared the frying pan and when it was hot enough I add the chopped onions. Then I added the chopped green, orange, red and yellow peppers. I stirred the peppers in the pan and checked on the mangu boiling. I loved cooking. I know my brothers were missing me right now. I made breakfast for them every morning. I fried six eggs. Cooking at Carlito house was easier. He had everything in the refrigerator. Carlito's refrigerator was 3

---

[13] ***Huevos criollos Dominicanos*** translates to fried eggs with a native twist.

[14] ***Mangu*** is mashed plantains a native specialty.

times bigger than my brothers' and 10 times bigger than the ice box my mother had. I added the finishing touches on the **huevos criollos Dominicanos** and mashed up the **mangu**. The coffee was last because it was the easiest. I boiled the beans and poured the boiled beans through a sock. I decorated the plate with the Dominican style breakfast. The aroma of the food called Carlito's zombie-like body to the kitchen. The first thing that caught my eye was his wide awake penis standing in the air. He walked over to me and wrapped his arms around my waist; bringing me closer to the standing penis. The words from his lips were words I would never forget. He said **"Despertar con tu Cara está viviendo un sueño**[15]**"** My eyes watered on his bare muscular chest. His caresses of consoling was a touch I hadn't felt in years. Yeah, my brothers definitely cared for me but they weren't the most **luvie dovie** [16]type of guys. After Carlito savagely

---

[15] **Despertar con tu cara está viviendo un sueño** translates to *"Waking up to your face is living a dream."*

gobbled down his breakfast he suggested I get the look of being his wife. He was taking me shopping. We drove into the pulse of the body of Dominican culture. This would be my second time going to the city part. I've lived on farm land all my 12 years of life. My brothers had introduced me to this different world, of stores, hotels and much more. My eyes couldn't soak it all up; it was so much movement. Our first stop was the beauty parlor. When me and Carlito fell through the door, mouths were silenced and eyes were locked on us. Carlito walked up to the owner, Gladie. "I want you personally to take care of her from head to toe." were Carlito's orders. Carlito explained away this acquaintance with Gladie with a friendship she shared between his mother. I looked in the mirror on the walls of the beauty parlor. There were no mirrors in my life my mother broke every single one in the house and cut up her legs. I stayed away from the truth that mirrors held, after seeing all that mirror's truth sparked.

---

[16] ***Luvie dovie*** *is Sistah's talk for affectionate.*

The image of my mother not being able to face the truth in herself keep me from mirrors. I was having a hard time looking at my truth. My hair was untamed and untreated. My body had more curves than the women in the parlor staring me down but it was covered in a child's outfit. Carlito fled the parlor leaving me in the hands of Gladie. First, my hair was washed but the shampoo girl was washing with flare. She couldn't hold back. She began to question me. "How old was I?" "How I knew Carlito?" "Where I came from?" she obviously had a thing for Carlito and I was proud to call him my husband. Every woman in the parlor jaws dropped. I sat under the hair dryer getting my nails and feet done at the same time. I felt like a million dollars. The envy in the women's eyes were a plus. Carlito arrived right in time; Gladie had just hard blown the last piece of hair. My hair fell to the middle of my back untamed but with my hair silky and shining it hit my waist line. Carlito returned with a sun dress on a hanger and a dozen of roses. He rushed me to the bathroom to change my clothes. The dress was a beautiful turquoise blue, it hugged by body. I thought maybe Carlito bought the wrong size but when I came out the bathroom and saw the women's eyes in the parlor pop out their heads I knew it was a perfect fit. I couldn't wait to get to the body sized mirror near the door in the parlor. I fell in love with the image. I was curse free. I could say goodbye to the cursed little girl and hello to the new woman. Carlito didn't say much while we were at lunch after we left the parlor. It was like he was back in the trance from last night. Apparently every man we passed was in the same trance. The sway in my hips and glow of my beauty had stolen the eyes of everyone, everywhere we walked. We spent the day walking and talking. Well I did most of the talking Carlito just nodded or spoke one word answers. He mainly was focused on hiding his wide awake penis that was poking out his pants. When we finally got home I was tired from the shopping. I had to try on all 30 dresses Carlito bought and the 30 shoes. The dresses and shoes transformed me to a little woman. Carlito cooked dinner while I showered and changed into the newly purchased sleep wear. The night gown was a light pink but completely see through. I would normally feel uncomfortable but Carlito had already seen me naked, so it wasn't a big deal. It was a wonderful day. I enjoyed the dinner cooked by Carlito hands. It was like we were in competition for best cook. Then the game from last night begun. Carlito kissed me from my forehead down to my stomach. My legs tensed up but didn't close. Carlito's pillow soft lips on my private parts were uncomfortable, it felt weird but I wanted to please him. He stopped and went to the awaiting teenaged girl in the living room. On this night Carlito pounded the teenaged girl insides while looking into my eyes and talking to me. "I want you" "I love you" were the words Carlito was saying to me. When he was done with the girl and a shower, we *crawled into bed together. Being wrapped in Carlito's arms all night equaled another night of curse-free nightmares. The third morning of being officially married to Carlito I was still happy and truly enjoying being curse free. We cooked breakfast together. Then he said he had a surprise and I should get dressed. I felt 8 again. I was rushing around. I hadn't had a pleasant surprise in years. My bright eyes were more than excited. We climbed into Carlito's car. The whole ride I played the guessing game trying to figure out the surprise. We ended up at his grandmother's house filled with Carlito's cousins, aunts and uncles and let's not forget Carlito's little sister Joanny. Joanny stared me up and down like a scorn lover. Everybody else played nice except her. Carlito checked her attitude but it only made it worst. Carlito instructed Joanny to teach me girly stuff. "Women don't parade around with hairy legs and armpits is first" "Second a Dominican wife should have make-up on" After Joanny belittled my appearance she taught me how* to shave and how to apply make-up to my face. She went the extra mile and trained me on how to walk in my 3 inch shoes, how to sit, and how to be intimate. She had educated me on the things a young girl should've learned from their mother. I was accustomed to just a pair of shorts a tee shirt and a pair of muddy **chanclas**[17], with my hair flying free in the air. I was a farm girl. Catching chickens, riding horses and eating fried **plátano**[18] sipping on a **malta**[19]. When I felt like it I played baseball just to show the so-called tough farm boys up. My brothers would bet on the sideline and make a profit off my showing off. But now I looked completely different and I felt different too. When Carlito eyes set on Joanny's girl-ing me up, his eyes fell to the wooden floor along with his jaw. He was stupefied. His grandmother called me over. She said

---

[17] **Chanclas** translates to flip flop tong sandals.

[18] **Plátano** translates to Latin banana.

[19] **Malta** is a Latin soft drink that contains five percent alcohol.

"Carlito had the pick of the best litters this county has to offer and he has chosen you over them all. You're a very special young lady, it's in your scent. You have seen more than your years and you shall see plenty more. But strength is in your blood you will survive it all. I will give my ring to you. Carlito has been trying to get this ring from me for years but I wouldn't give it to just anyone except the one and you are the one. Here is the ring that my husband saved to buy it's 100 percent real gold and real diamonds." Carlito placed the ring on my right ring finger and the make-up that took hours to learn how to put on was now running down my cheek with tears. Carlito's grandmother made it seem like an honor to be the wife of Carlito. I felt like a winner and I hadn't won in a long time. I went to the bathroom and fixed what I messed up. This time Joanny stood outside the bathroom, I was on my own. I took my time, applying the eye shadow then the eyeliner, then the blush on my cheeks, last but not least the lipstick. I know I did a good job, Joanny was clapping and jumping up and down. Carlito's eyes screamed excitement along with the bulge poking out of his pants. I walked up on him and planted my painted lips on top of his and stuck my tongue in his mouth like he had done to me. He had a grin plastered on his face the whole ride home. The third day ended with Carlito sitting in the chair; the same chair I sat in to watch him handle the teenaged girl in our living room. He was watching my nude body walk back and forth, bend over and squat. Ironically that's exactly what the c.o.s (correctional officers) are currently doing to me right now. Anyway he watched me walk while he used his right hand to stroke his awakened penis. His eyes locked on my beauty. The strokes intensified as I walked my nude body over to him. I leaned down and kissed him as he had kissed me from his forehead down to his stomach. Before I knew it, the cream that is usually on the teenaged girl was on my breast. We showered together and I slept a *good night in his arms. On the fourth morning, my brothers woke us up by banging on the door. Carlito ran to open the door. They had breakfast with them. We ate, laughed and joked. Carlito decided to go to the gym with my brothers and I was to stay home. My argument was I always went to the gym why couldn't I go today. My brothers excused themselves and I was left to deal with Carlito. I was expecting my brothers to side with me but being Carlito's wife meant they were to mind their business. Carlito had never raised his voice toward me. I've seen Carlito get straight up ugly on other men at the gym but to me, never. As he yelled his face changed and the charm disappeared and the touch of fear had entered our relationship. I stood behind. I cleaned the house and cooked dinner and then showered. Then I dressed up in one of the night gowns Carlito bought and a pair of heels. I made up my face and mind. I wanted to be the teenage girl that was under Carlito. Tonight it was my turn. Carlito walked in the* door apologetic. He expressed how pleased he was with the food and my appearance. He didn't have to say a word I could read the excitement in his pants. Tonight was different Carlito kisses were gentle and patient not lustful. After kissing on my private area he waited for confirmation to proceed. I claimed to be ready. He didn't do me like he did the teenage girl. He inched his penis into me. He put the head in and out until my private adjusted. Once adjusted, he would add a little more. Each add in I could hear my privates ripping. It was a burning sensation. When it cooled to his stroke he would heat up again by adding more of himself inside of me. When he finally got the whole penis in me the cream filled me. I rushed to the bathroom. In the light I could see the blood run down my legs. My insides burned just as much as the outside. A cold shower cooled the outside but the inside needed rest. I went back to the room and Carlito was changing the sheets; there was blood on the sheets. The fifth day was a day of total rest. I never left the bed. Today, Carlito had cooked breakfast, lunch and dinner. I showered because it was showtime. Carlito couldn't and wouldn't go to sleep without getting pleasure to his penis. And I was willing to give Carlito what he wanted. He fed and pampered me the entire day. He even rubbed my feet. I didn't care too much for the nights of him thrusting in and out of my private area but I did love his heavy breathing in my ear. His passionate 'I loves you's were music to my ears. The next morning we had breakfast in the city area of DR. Then we went to an office to apply for our passports. While waiting; there was an older woman shouting about waiting 3 years for her passport and still had nothing. She was demanding her money back. Carlito paid the extra money to get express service. 2 months of Carlito's night time game equaled to Edwin growing in my stomach. A **comadrona** [20] had come to live in the house with me and Carlito. The elder woman

---

[20] **Comadrona** translates to midwife.

cooked, cleaned and tended to me. I would lay in the bed all day and have sex with Carlito all night. Giving birth was 10 times the pain of sex with Carlito. I knew there was a baby inside of me because I felt him move. But when he actually busted out of my private I was amazed. Comadrona stitched my privates back together after Edwin's grand entrance into this world. She also had to stand guard because Carlito's trance of my beauty couldn't keep his hands or penis away from me. But she failed miserably I was pregnant again in two months with Pedro. Being pregnant with Pedro was harder than being pregnant with Edwin. I was sick every day and instead of gaining weight I was losing. Comadrona cared for me until it was time to give birth. She was afraid to deliver Pedro. Carlito took me to a hospital in the city area. I knew my stay was costing him a pretty penny. The nurse was so kind; it was like having 4 Comadronas around. It was a pleasant vacation from Carlito's penis. Besides the pains of Pedro's entrance into the *world, the hospital was a break. With Edwin it was a natural birth, no medication but with Pedro I was doped up to the max and it was still more excruciating than Edwin. Pedro is still a pain in my ass today, even though we only talk once every three months for the last 9 years. Our relationship has be this way since he decided he was too much of a man to listen to the rules of my home, so he left to live with Carlito at 18. Then to see how he physically and mentally broke that woman, I want to beat his ass. I really didn't believe in hitting on kids after what my mother put me through, but Pedro would push that button every time. Edwin would follow Pedro around. I could never figure out why Edwin never took his role as the oldest. They are 11 months apart. At 13 I had 2 sons and was pregnant again. And the passports still hadn't been processed. Carlito was deep into illegal business now trying to feed us all. His real money was in America and to get it we needed the passports. I went to my brothers and they had extras to give toward the* family, my mistake for accepting. Carlito busted my lip for begging. He also busted my heart; he had never raised his voice since that day years ago much less a hand. He of course apologized. Miguel was a quiet pregnancy. I would eat ice just to make sure he was still alive. I was petrified the whole 8 months. Miguel came early. In no time Edwin and Pedro were 2 years old. Miguel was 1 and I was 14 years old and you guessed it, pregnant again. Carlito was now 24 years old. Whatever he was doing was working I now had **niñera**[21] and a Comadrona. I didn't ask no questions; not because it was forbidden for a wife to second guess her husband but because I just was too young to care. I was a mother of 3, barefoot and pregnant. My life was an adult but my mind was 15 years old. Pedro would lead Edwin into all types of mischief. These two adored Carlito. Carlito would take them on errands, just like Papi had done me. I always wondered did they stop by Carlito's other

---

[21] **Niñera** *translates to female babysitter.*

women's houses. Did Carlito have other children like Papi had? I wondered but didn't dare ask. Miguel was a good quiet baby and an even excellent quieter toddler. He played in one spot and one spot only. Miguel was always left behind. Carlito said "The boy don't have any fight in him." Miguel didn't care too much for Carlito either; he kinda lingered at my side. My 15th birthday was one to remember I gave birth to Dino the last installment to E.P.M.D. and the top of the day we received notice that our passport applications had been approved. At me and Carlito's house it was like Sunday dinners at home with my mother and Papi. Carlito announced that Dino was his last child. He fired Comadrona in front of his family but Ninera was given permission to stay. I had just given birth a few hours after ***mensajero*** [22] left us with the news that we had documentation leading to the states. Carlito had a tendency to just be rude after a few shots of ***Brugal Añejo*** [23] and he was rude the

---

[22] ***Mensajero*** translates to Messenger.

whole day. From Carlito's intoxicated lips I learned about the fatal gun shot to Jorge. In my young mind it was of an act of love from Carlito but I later learned Jorge's life was ended over drugs and had nothing to do with me at all. The states was a chance to alter my life. I was grateful for the news of the states. I looked forward to the states. Carlito promised a future for the boys. I wanted them to have the opportunity to go to school. They would have the chance to be more than just what was expected; a farmer, a father or a just a far memory in faded pictures. I wanted them to be more than an average Dominican dreamer, wishing on a baseball or boxing ring. I begged Carlito to cancel the birthday party after giving birth but he wouldn't hear of it. "It's a call for a celebration, we have freedom to leave this dirt and grass for streets and sidewalks, and my fourth son was born and today is your birthday. The party goes on!" the party did

---

[23] ***Brugal* Añejo** is one hundred forty three proof Dominican rum, in the United States it's sold at forty three proof.

go on and it didn't stop the night time games. Carlito had used my body as my insides to release his pleasure cream. The next morning after my birthday, I had ninera get Comadrona to sew my private area back close. Carlito's animalistic sexual drive had busted 5 stitches. I must've been to tired or too over joyed with Dino being born that I missed the excruciating pain that came with the sewing. Over time I was more into giving sexual pleasure to Carlito, knowing that another kid wasn't going to come from it. The next two years went by like a breeze, Joanny practically moved into our house. She was hating from the door. Carlito hired a **cocinero** [24] *and ninera was still living with us. "Who marries a wife that don't cook, clean or tend to her own children?" Carlito shut her down by saying "I don't want her to wear out her beauty; my beautiful wife will live worry free." I was 17 years old, Edwin and Pedro were 5, Miguel 4 and my sweet Dino 3. Dino took a liking to me. He would*

---

[24] **Cocinero** translates to a cook.

brush my hair and kiss my hand, face, or eye where ever his little lips would land. **"Eres mi amigo**[25]**?"** was Dino's favorite question all day long. Pedro would make him cry by answering "No". Carlito would have sex with me in the morning, have breakfast with me and the boys and then leave. Then Carlito would come back at lunchtime, have sex, have lunch with me and the boys and leave again. He would then come back at dinnertime have dinner with me and the boys and have sex all night long. I often wondered where he got the energy. A day with the boys, me and niñera would be wore out. I learned later on that Carlito's energy source were in white lines. Carlito was making money off the coffee bean farm we owned and his illegal business. He had money flow from the shady business with José Louié. And other business, I tried to stay out of it. Finally the passports were ready and we were packing to head off to New York. After waiting 5 years for me and

---

[25] **Eres mi amigo?** translates to "Are you my friend?"

Carlito's passports they did all four of the boys right there on the spot for 600 dollars each. Carlito slapped the money down on the table. I had four kids and the office clerk behind the desk couldn't keep his eyes off my beauty. I snapped back into my shape I had when I was 12 years old magnificently. Carlito was insanely jealous. I had just caught a peek when he slammed the money down to break the clerk's stares with 'ease by you' eyes. I am not going to tell no lies I started welcoming the attention. Carlito had sex with me three times a day but he didn't compliment me or make me over like in the beginning. He still fell into the trance when I was nude but that was the only thing from the past in the present. Carlito had family already situated in New York. I wanted to see the place I was named after. My mother's closest friend Anaya was shipped to family in Brooklyn. Anaya's parents were killed in a car accident in DR. My mother missed and loved her friend. I know because she kept the letters that turned into cards, which turned *into memories. To honor her friend's freedom from being an average Dominican wife I was named after the place Anaya called home. Papi hated the idea but fell to my mother's story. New York here comes the Cruz."*

Retrospective of the refection, defective affection.

The bar is a wooden rail barrier, separating court officials from the public. The wooden court pews are seasoned with family, friends and Sistahs', waiting on news of their incarcerated loved one. Rhonda and Sammy are no different they are waiting for the court clerk to shout Brooklyn's docket number.

"Ladies a moment, please?" Marquez Ortiz, attorney at law is requesting Rhonda and Sammy's presence in the court house hallway. The Sistahs' follow his lead.

Rhonda and Sammy had puzzled faces. They didn't know the man but followed his expensive navy blue pinstriped suit.

Rhonda's eyes were glued to the man's **Slick dick** [26] scent of cologne.

"I've been retained as Brooklyn's criminal defense lawyer. I just spoke to Brooklyn. She is claiming her innocence. Today I'm going to present the judge with a **case severance**[27]. If it is approved then I can get her out in a week. There's a small manner of this court appearance fee that hasn't been resolved. I was told by my employer that you lovely ladies will be compensating me?"

"Who gave that false information?" Rhonda questions Marquez with her body gesture and hand movement.

---

[26] *Slick Dick* in Sistah's talk is an older man with the mannerisms of young man.

[27] *Case severance* is a legal term for co-defendants to be trail separately.

"My employer prefers to remain nameless. With my employer covering the retainer fee, he didn't see it being a problem with you ladies chipping in on your friend's freedom. Do we have a deal?"

"How much are we talking?" Sammy asks, revealing her willingness to pay any reasonable price to grant Brooklyn's freedom.

"5 thousand per appearance. Ladies I can assure you I will have this case sewn up in no time. You are not dealing with an amateur."

"We have a deal. Now can we talk about the case? I read the public court file she is being charged with a felony arson charge. What was the property that was damaged? Was someone injured? Was someone killed?" Sammy's concern spit out into questions being fired at Marquez.

"Yes property was damaged and the victim has filed a statement wanting jail time and restitution. A Mrs. Crystal Moore, is actively pursuing some form of punishment. Brooklyn has been charged with Arson in the second degree, which is a class B felony. The state of New York has sentenced a man to 50 years for the same crime but if I can get her case severance the co-defendant is admitting guilt. Brooklyn would have to testify as a witness. But she might still have to pay the victim off."

"Crystal is always more trouble than she's worth. I wonder why Brooklyn would even entertain Kamal Campbell's bullshit." Rhonda's chitachatter escapes her head and flows from her lips.

"Kamal was hurt by Crystal so I can understand why he did what he did but Brooklyn is a more in your face type of bitch, setting fires just doesn't sound like her. I wish we could talk to Brooklyn to get the whole story. It's too many holes but Brooklyn can't keep her ass outta the hole." Sammy gathers her thoughts verbally.

"Well let's get back inside before they call her case number." Marquez suggests.

Marquez leads Rhonda and Sammy back into the court room. He takes his seat in the front pew, seating persevered for lawyers. The bailiff is the court officer and stands guard at the bar. The criminal court room on the fifth floor is boxed in by three wooden walls and a wall of two enormous windows. The Judge sits on the bench in the front of the room, in the traditional black robe. His reading glasses sit on his nose as he rereads the court document in his right hand. Above the judge's head hanging on the wall, is a large plaque reading the logo of the dollar bill "In God We Trust." On the left and right side of the judge's sides are two American flags. Adjacent to the judge's bench is the witness stand. Desks where the court clerk and court stenographer sits is in front of the Judge's desk. The lectern is in front of the court clerk's desk. The lectern is where the prosecution positions themselves to address the judge. There is one table behind the lectern. The table is for the defendant. On the right side of the defendant table are two rows of wooden benches. The benches are covered with inmates covered in bright orange jumpsuits with the twelve inch initials "D.O.C" on the back. Next to the witness box is the door where the inmates enter and exit the court room. Brooklyn emerges from the inmates doors. Her hands are handcuffed in front of her, which in connected to her brown leather belt around her waist, the cuffs around her ankle has a long chain also connected to the brown leather belt. Brooklyn is heavily supervised by a court officer on her right and another on her left.

"Damn, what they did to Bk? She's looking like eighteen again, with cornrows to the back. The look she rocking right now is the look the Sistahs' gave her. I met Bk in '89. When I was fucking with a nicca named Kemo, from the heights. See back then it was about what you had and what nicca you were fucking to get it. Crack cocaine owned New York City's streets and who was getting rich or who was getting poor of it were the only people known. And to be known was to be on a throne. I was a queen riding shot gun

in Kemo's snow white MPV minivan with the tan bottom rim, seating gold rims and tinted windows. Couldn't tell me nuttin, I was 17 pretending to be 18 with my skin tight stone washed Edwin jeans that held my fat ass up right, shit I was turning heads everywhere I went. But back then this ass was for sale to the highest hustler. That was just the rules of the game and I was playing; shit all the Sistahs' were players. And I had Jordan's; number 4's on my feet thanks to Kemo. See the difference from today's number 4 Jordan's and 1989 Jordan's was the hint of yellow on the back of the sole, but the $110 price tag is still the same. My hair, yes back then I had hair, was laid. I had gotten a wash, set and doobie hairstyle from Gomez's; which was the popular Dominican owned beauty parlor on 2nd ave. Everybody from the hood went to Gomez's. Back then following trend was the in thing to do. And I was all the way in. I had 5 inch 14 karat gold door knocker earrings, thanks again to Kemo. Kemo originated from east Harlem but bought, cooked and bottled his cocaine turned to crack on 150th street and Broadway at his cousin, bowlegged Jackie's 5th floor apartment. Me and Jackie were kicked out of the apartment while product production was in play. Kemo would hand over a fist full of money to keep me busy while he worked. Me and Jackie had shopped around Broadway, then went to the roof of Jackie's building to smoke a few joints. While we were up in the roof getting high; out of nowhere a girl climbed over the edge of the building off the fire escape in a fire red Dominican sequence party dress with a toddler on the front of her body. The toddler was holding on to her neck. The girl scared the shit outta me. I thought it was police coming for me or even Kemo. The girl was Brooklyn. I was trying to find out where she came from, but she didn't speak English. Thank goodness Jackie was half Dominican and half black. The Dominican half was able to translate somewhat. Brooklyn was escaping Carlito's cocaine induced jealous *rage by climbing out her 5th floor apartment window, up the fire escape to the roof with her 2 year old son, Dino holding on to her neck with his legs crossed behind her back. Jackie got Brooklyn to relax. I immediately took a liking to Brooklyn; she had only been in the United States for a month. For the next 5 months me and Jackie dedicated our Friday nights to rooftop jokes, smoke and talks with Brooklyn. We taught her English, while they both taught me Spanish. I learned some of her stories from DR to NY. I pitied Brooklyn she had no clue that 17 with 4 kids and a 27 year old cocaine head husband wasn't all life had to offer. I wanted to free her but her loyalty to Carlito was stronger than my words. "* Rhonda's chitachatter is actively running through her head.*

Brooklyn stands still but her eyes and mind wanders over the public pews filled with family. She spots Rhonda and Sammy. A sense of relief soothes her mind. Before the feeling of relief could settle in her blood, the court doors flew open, the sight made Brooklyn's blood begin to boil. Nobody else would make a grand entrance at a criminal court room but Crystal, with a hazelnut coated **tender bone**[28] at her side. Crystal's grand entrance caught the eye and tongues of everyone in the court room.

"This bitch does the most." Rhonda voiced her annoyance in a loud whisper to Sammy.

"Her presence is so unnecessary." Sammy replies.

Brooklyn's eyes are locked on Crystal's all white attire but sees straight into her black heart. Brooklyn's stare is broken by the court clerk shouting out her docket number.

---

[28] **Tender bone** *in Sistah talk is a men with a gentleman posture, confidence and excellent bedroom skills.*

The two officers at her stand escorted her to stand before the judge. The officers stood back to allow Marquez Ortiz to stand at her side.

"Your honor, case severance, Kamal Campbell, the co-defendant has admitted guilt, my client was just at the wrong place at the wrong time." Marquez pleads Brooklyn's case to the judge.

"Does the prosecution accept the defendant's request?" The judge asks.

"Yes, your honor, we the people request that the defendant pleads to a less charge of negligence."

"Defense attorney is accepting the less charge?" the judge questions Marquez Ortiz.

After Brooklyn and Marquez whisper back and forth, Marquez agrees to the prosecution's request. The two officers regain position at Brooklyn's side and within seconds, Brooklyn was returning to the door that she entered in. Brooklyn looked back at Rhonda and Sammy.

"A piece of pie." Brooklyn shouts the expresses her desire to have an American life in over her shoulder.

"A piece of ass." Rhonda shouts her request for a sexual snack sexual as Brooklyn in spite of the Bailiff's dirty look.

"A piece of solitude." Sammy shouts her signature wish for inner self peace.

Brooklyn's words were shouted into the air to ease the worried look on the Sistahs" faces. The four little words had put the Sistahs" hearts at ease as their words did the same for Brooklyn. The Sistahs' created this wishing game on Magdalena's rooftop years ago. The wishes graduated into be a Sistah's greeting, farewell, promise or just words to soothe the soul of the Sistahs' in time of need. The Sistahs"   immediately followed Marquez outside the court room doors. Their inquiring minds needed and wanted to know the next step toward Brooklyn's release.

"Well ladies today was a win. Now I have to get her on the court calendar to get her released. I am going downstairs to make that happen right now. Samantha I'll call you with the date once I get it." Marquez explains his movements.

"How far away will the next court date be?"

"I'm going to get the closest date possible."

"Okay and at the next court day she'll be released?" Rhonda questions

"She should be. I have never seen someone be held for a misdemeanor charge."

As the Sistahs' thank Marquez for his service, Crystal enters the court hallway with her with a hazelnut coated tender bone.

"It's a civil case to get her to pay for the damages, but with the lesser charge it's going to be hard to make the civil case stick, but I will still file the paper work, it doesn't hurt to try." The hazelnut coated tender bone lawyer explains to Crystal.

"Sammy, why can't you keep a handle on your wild animals? Last month Chyenne's weak ass hit me and now your jungle bunny has burned down my mansion. Can the Sistahs' just get over me?" Crystal's thin upper lips spits out words with her distinguished superior tone.

Crystal's words made Rhonda jump with her fist balled up. Sammy places her hand on Rhonda's shoulder.

"She ain't worth it." Sammy's words reminded Rhonda of why hitting Crystal was a wrong idea.

"Ce n'est pas ce que vous voulez![29]" Crystal's words fell from her thin upper lip in a light chuckle.

"You know what Crystal? You walk around wit your head in the clouds looking down on everybody you pass shouting your French words but Sistah you're from the same gutter as the rest of us. So what you have money, it can't buy personality and character; the two main things you are lacking." Sammy reads Crystal.

"The part that boils me is that WE know your uppity ass while you pretending to be somebody else! I know why you act like that you miss us!" Rhonda exposes Crystal's inner feelings as she sees it.

---

[29] *Ce n'est pas ce que vous voulez* Translates to "This ain't what you want" from French to English.

"Miss who? These hood boogers have lost their mind." Crystal's chitachatter.

Crystal storms off with her Lawyer. Rhonda couldn't help but to continue taking second and third looks at Crystal's lawyer. Marquez ushers the Sistahs' out the court building. He voiced different variations of what could happen. The Sistahs' left the building well educated on Brooklyn's case. Rhonda would relay the information to Le'Roy while Sammy was on her way to regurgitate her knowledge to Dino, Brooklyn's youngest but the most sensitive to his mother's current situation. Brooklyn was put into a holding cell in the court building. In the cell Brooklyn's body was caged but her mind ran free into her past.

"Carlito's whole family saw us off to the states at the airport in DR. My beautiful brothers received my farewell kisses and tears. My tears were flowing from the

thought of missing my brothers but feeling that hadn't come yet. I cried because it was the end of Cocinero and Niñera. It wasn't that I didn't like to cook I was just spoiled. I didn't have to so I didn't want to. The boys were a different story. Niñera had her hands filled with Edwin and Pedro. They did everything under the sun. If there was mischief, they found or created some. She was always chasing after them. Dino stayed at my side and Miguel was so quiet, I would often forget he was around. Joanny was great entertainment. I would miss her shady attitude. She had a way of using her words to crawl under my skin. "Tell **muñeca** [30] *I said hi." Joanny shouted the words to Carlito's back but the words slapped me in the face. Who the hell was* **muñeca**? *The question rolled around in my head the whole plane ride. I had never been on a plane before; my nerves were flying high and I wanted to question Carlito but I just couldn't bring my lips to perform the job. I was more*

---

[30] **Muñeca** *translates to baby doll*

nervous than the boys but I tried to be strong for them. Carlito bought our tickets on the discount so our seats were spread around the plane. Me and Dino sat side by side, you know he would have it no other way. I had a window seat. I watched DR go from small to ant size to completely disappearing. Through the window I saw my old life, the curse and the pain disappeared like my homeland did in my eyes. Goodbye to the old cursed me. As the plane flew above the clouds; my mind flew into them and I imagined a brighter and better life awaiting me. It was an honor to be Carlito's wife but I wondered more about what my life would become. I looked over at Carlito. I noticed I wasn't the only one nervous. His skin was sweating profusely. His eyes were bulging. His mouth was dry, I could tell because his lips were white. I had fear for his health. I called the Stewardess over to assist Carlito. The boys were the calmest of us all. The plane landed on states soil the beginning of June in the year of 1989. Marquez Ortiz's driver was awaiting *our arrival. He stood patiently waiting with his fingers peeking out on the sides of a big white sign with huge black letters spelling out Cruz. The driver escorted Carlito, our four boys and myself to a black limo. In the back seat of the limo sat Marquez. Marquez handed Carlito a tiny folded paper. Carlito quickly unfolded the paper and inhaled the insides of the paper. At the time I had no idea what he was doing but Rhonda broke it down to me later on. I was just clueless. Carlito had convinced me that the powder he inhaled was medicine for his headaches and not his addiction. Marquez was breaking down the hoops Carlito had to jump through to get to his father's money. First he had to marry pure, and by pure that meant a woman had to be full Dominican blood and a virgin. I passed the marriage requirements. Then the next thing was to get to the states to claim the money. Just getting into states took five years. Now Carlito had to become a United States citizen to gain access to the money. And to become a USA citizen you* need a green card. To get a green card, one had to live in the USA for 3 years. As the words of direction fell from Marquez's lips the frustration was bending Carlito's eyebrows inward. Marquez started talking fast. He quickly explained that he had a green card already with his name on it. Marquez eased Carlito's eyebrows back in place. All Carlito had to do was take a test and attend the ceremony all in English. Marquez had already had the English classes all lined up. "Where is my love Muñeca?" I was half listening until I heard Carlito speak in English and that name "Muñeca" being thrown in the air again rocked my soul. My mind was at tug-a-war with all types of questions. Did Carlito marry me based off of our connection or was it just a step closer to his father's money? Who the fuck was this Muñeca? Once or twice I've caught Carlito crying over a drink whispering the same name... Muñeca. I had always thought he was hurting from a loss but it never crossed my mind it was tears for a miss. I fought with these questions for years and never truly gotten the answers I wanted or could face. After the long ride and talk Marquez's driver dropped us off on 150th and Broadway after a brief meeting with Carlito's mother, Ana 1st floor apartment on 104th and 1st ave. We were at Ana's house all of 10 minutes. She looked the boys over. **"No hay duda que son sus hijos"**[31] was the words that flew from her wrinkled lips. We were there 10 minutes too long. Bitch! On 150th street it was crowded with abandoned bodies, buildings and kids. The abandoned bodies' souls had left them and what was left was a bunch of crack heads. The burnt buildings were abandoned by the inexperience crack cookers. The only thing left was a shell of a once lived in building with charcoal colored boarded up windows decorated with spray painted nick names. Parents had abandoned these kids; leaving them to fend for themselves. The fast moving

---

[31] **No hay duda que son sus hijos** translates to "There's no doubt these are your sons."

bodies, burnt buildings and unattended children was all new to me. I was soaking up the crowded vacated scenery. Carlito lead the way up the 6 steps into the tenement building and then up 5 flights, of 10 more steps, to the top floor. We passed more deserted bodies, sexual activity and a million tiny glass bottles with multi-colored caps decorating the floor, from the lobby to the apartment door on the fifth floor. Before I stepped foot into the apartment I was already home sick. I was already missing the familiarity of faces, the sweet clean air and of course the hundred degree weather. Carlito's aunt, Magdalena, was holding the door open for us. She was anticipating our arrival. "El alquiler es pagadero el 1 de cada mes! Cualquiera de conseguir un trabajo o venderle culo, si usted necesita ayuda con la venta de culo, puede asisto, pero la renta se debe a la primera que no sí ands o peros al respecto!" These were the words that flew from her lips as she planted kisses on Carlito, me and the boys. What she said *translated in English was "Rent is due on the 1st of every month! Either get a job or sell your ass, if you need help with selling ass, I can assist, but rent is due on the 1st no if ands or but's about it!!!" Whether it was said in English or Spanish it was still disrespectful. My 1ˢᵗ states lesson was "everything ain't what it seems". It seemed like Magdalena was happy for her family's arrival but her words made it clear that this was a business arrangement among family. She guided us to a box called a room. I thought the tiny room was for the boys but in fact the room was for all of us. Six people in such a small space was definitely a mistake. There wasn't enough breathing room in there. I immediately expressed my discomfort but was silenced by the back of Carlito's hand. The hit wasn't strong but had shocked me motionless. This was the second time Carlito talked to my lips with his hands. He apologized a second after the hit, nonetheless I was amazed at how quick he was on the draw. He explained it away with* the hoops he had and would continue to jump through to get the money that was due to him. We had been traveling all day long and it was now nine o'clock at night. I was hungry and I knew the boys were starving. Carlito settled us in the room and went out to hunt for our food. He returned 2 hours later with a bag of uncooked rice, a can of goya beans and a can of corn beef. I had the puzzled look plastered on my face. How the fuck was I gonna cook a meal at 11 o'clock at night? ***"Siempre que tengo una esposa, yo y mis hijos a tener una comida casera"*** [32] Carlito's words flew from his lips but the strength behind the words were impacted in his wide eyes. I didn't hesitate; I rushed to the kitchen to begin dinner at 11 o'clock at night. This was the beginning of me doing things because Carlito said it and not because it made sense. I got into the kitchen and everything was under lock and key. The

---

[32] ***"Siempre que tengo una esposa, yo y mis hijos a tener una comida casera*** translates to "As long as I have a wife, me and my sons will have a home cooked meal".

cabinet and refrigerator were all locked. I walked back down the hallway in the apartment toward our room but stopped at the room door on the left side of our room and knocked. Magdalena swung the door open with an irritated look in her eyes. I explained my dilemma. "Cocina cercana a las diez, pero ya que es su primera noche te voy a dar un descanso, y es cinco dólares por usar mis ollas y sartenes, usted va a pagar ahora o debo añadido a la renta?" Her words were clear in Spanish and even more clear in English "Kitchen closes at ten but since it's your first night I'll give you a break, and it's five dollars for using my pots and pans, you going to pay now or should I add it to the rent?" is what she said in English. She was gonna have to add it to the rent because there was no way in hell I was gonna return to that room without Carlito's plate of food asking for 5 dollars. I followed her lead into the kitchen. Once the cabinets were open and Magdalena was outta my way, I got busy. I put the pot of rice on the stove. I fried the can *of corn beef and then added the beans with a dash of spices. When I returned to the room; the boys and Carlito were wide eyed cause their stomachs were awake. They scraped their paper plates clean. My weak eyes won over my stomach. I had fallen asleep awaiting one of the kids to finish so I could eat off the plate. Magdalena was so generous to have given us 2 plates and 2 forks for a small fee. Or maybe my eyes closed to block out the painful sight of my sons eat off a plate with their hands like back farm dogs. Each one of them bumping, pushing and snarling for a handful of food of the plate. But my sleep was disturbed by Carlito's cold fingers playfully touching my private parts at 3 a.m. I pretended to still be asleep. Not only was I not willing to have sex in front of my kids, but after today I truly wasn't in the mood. Would you wanna have sex after traveling from DR to the States, sitting in the back of a car for over an hour, climbing up sixty steps with four toddlers and luggage, being slapped and then cooking* dinner? And lets not forget the muñeca business, cus' I didn't! Shit, I'm tired by just repeating the recap of the day. Me being pretend sleep meant absolutely nothing to Carlito, he slipped his manhood right up in me with no regards for the boys. I couldn't fall asleep after Carlito was finished pleasing himself with my body. My mind had questions. I wanted to know did we really make the right decision? We were sleeping on the floor of an apartment when we lived comfortably in a house. Paying for pots and pans? This was nowhere close to what was promised by Carlito's lips. Carlito went to the bathroom and returned with the news of the sangre. I was more than happy for the sangre but it didn't stop Carlito from wanting more of me. Dino picked his head up with his eyes filled with tears. It was five a.m. the next morning and Dino was looking for his morning warm bottle of milk. Carlito's solution was "lo dejó llorar, un hombre debe tener buenos pulmones, además de que no he terminado contigo todavía" Carlito's suggestion was to "let him cry, a man should have strong lungs, plus I'm not finished with you yet." When he was finally done, there was blood all over the floor bed. Magdalena quickly suggested I go to the hospital. Carlito wouldn't hear of it. He insisted that we would keep to our tradition and call a **Curandera**[33]. Now you know I've had my share of them fucking Curanderas. I was all for Magdalena's idea and wanted to go to the hospital. There was no telling what fucked up prediction would flow from a Curandera's mouth this time. I've been curse free for 5 years I wasn't in the mood for some back wood analysis. Me and Magdalena were simply ignored. Carlito called on a Curandera against my wishes. Cuandera's prediction was that I had carried death inside beauty. The lost of life had had taken place in my body. And dead life in such beauty would bring death to those around me. Magdalena claimed she didn't believe in Cuandera's words but still gave us 6 months to stay in

---

[33] **Curandera** *translates to female healer.*

her apartment. Where was my Carlito? My Carlito, who would put the boys' needs above his own desires. Carlito started to look different to me. His skin color, the set of his lips and his touch was all too unfamiliar. My Carlito wouldn't have sex with me while our 1 year old son cried in my arms. My Carlito didn't grunt and groan loud enough to wake up the boys that were sleeping. My Carlito wouldn't allow me to cook. My Carlito promised a worry free life. I had lost the Carlito I loved to the tiny folded paper and another curse was hanging over my head. Carlito was gone all day long leaving me cooped up in that room with the boys. The 1st week in the states was a heat wave, and there was no fan in our room. One day I went out on the fire escape for air. I was people watching. All the abandoned kids of the area were playing in the fire hydrant. They were laughing and enjoying themselves under the false rain drops. I stared at their faces and wished I had enjoyed my youth just like them at this moment. My day dream was interrupted by Edwin's cries. Pedro had punched him in the arm again. Dino started crying just 'cause Edwin was crying. Dino felt the pain for all his brothers. If one cried he cried. Carlito would come and go as he pleased. When he left and didn't return I would find blame within myself. And when he returned I showered him with unwanted affection. Things had changed. I always felt like I was doing something wrong. The closer I thought I was getting to Carlito the further I truly was. After a month of being a prisoner to the rooms' walls, Carlito returned with "great news" he claimed. He had purchased a bodega. I was so angry. How could he afford to buy a store when we didn't even have a home? Where did the money come from? He hadn't finished jumping through hoops to get his father's money. See, I know now he was utilizing my families' money but back then I had no idea. He wanted me and the boys to see his store. He was so overjoyed that I laid my questions to the side to enjoy Carlito's moment. The moment was tainted by Muñeca. Muñeca was the counter girl. She was beautiful in states's clothing. My eyes dropped to the floor. She was close to Carlito's age. I had a million and one questions for her but they were all answered when Muñeca and Carlito locked eyes. Between their eyes something special was shared between them. Carlito had dropped me and boys back off at Magdalena's apartment after announcing he would be working late at the bodega. After walking up all the stairs, I began dinner, fed the boys and laid them down for bed. Pedro was 5 years old. Pedro had a rebellious soul. Whatever I said Pedro did the opposite. I told him to eat he took a shower, I told him to shower he began to eat. And Edwin followed Pedro's every move. Miguel was sweet and quiet. He followed directions and never talked back. Dino sensed something was wrong with me so he stood up by my side. Dino was only 3 years old with the mind of a protector. I stood up all night around 1 am, Magdalena knocked on the room door. She *offered me a cup of tea and conversation. I guess she heard me pacing backing and forth in the room. I knew where Carlito was, but what he was doing was keeping me away from sleep. Magdalena was very informational. Muñeca was born in the states but when she found herself pregnant at 17 years old, she was shipped to DR. She lived in DR during her pregnancy, gave birth, sold the baby and moved back to the states. The year in DR was enough time for Muñeca to have stolen Carlito's heart. She also broke it when she came back to the states. She killed his spirit when news came back to DR that she had married. Magdalena ended her story by saying Muñeca was Carlito's one and only true love. I felt like I had been living a complete lie for the last 5 years. Did Carlito use me to get back to his precious Muñeca? The story left a bad taste in my heart for Carlito. Magdalena had more information about Edwin and Pedro being put in daycare. Daycare would get them ready for September, when they would start public* school. She said I could even go to school. I thought I was too old for school. Magdalena enlightened me that in the states I was never too old for school. She was willing to help me with getting the boys into school and then she would work on me. I was filled with mixed feelings... I hated Carlito for not being what he appeared to be and happy to be finally being around other 17 year old females like myself. Carlito didn't come back to Magdalena's house. I waited til' 5 am and nothing. At 9 am the next day; me and Magdalena went and got Edwin, Pedro and Miguel into daycare, Dino was old enough to be enrolled but he wasn't ready to leave his mother's side. I had 2 months to get him ready. September would be here in no time. And in September I was going to be a student at Washington Irving High School. We had a long day. I was happy to return to my box of a room. Still no sign of Carlito. Me and the boys was awakened by a new family moving into the room on the right side of my room. It was two brothers from DR., Daniel and

Steven Ortega. They didn't have anything but the clothes on their backs. Their stomach and hands were empty. So when I cooked dinner I made enough to feed me, the boys, Daniel and Steven. My days were different now. I got up early to feed the boys and dropped them off at daycare; that was three blocks up and two blocks across. I would practice numbers and letters with Dino. We were learning English together. Dino was my joy. In this new world all I had was Dino and his pure love. It amazed me how the love from a 3 year old was the only thing I needed and wanted. It was a whole week since I laid eyes on Carlito. Carlito had left a sock in the room with $150 in it, after a week I was down to $25. I spent $100 on just putting the boys in daycare for three weeks I was gonna need another $100 to keep them in. Daniel was my age and his brother also left him alone. Me, Daniel and Dino would climb to the roof of the building from the fire escape outside my room window. On the roof I would sun bathe, have water fights with

Daniel and Dino, or just play around with Dino. It was two weeks since I had seen Carlito and I was down to $5. Me and the boys would have been living off just rice if it wasn't for Daniel. Daniel had made $50 off of cashing in cans and bottles. One morning around 3 am. Carlito crawled through the door. He obviously had been drinking Brugal Añejo and inhaling powder. It was dripping off his breath. I was awakened by him pulling my hair to bring me to my feet and pinning me to the wall. His actions immediately woke up Dino, who was sleeping in my arms. He was screaming out "*Tu coño es tan caliente que mierda en la casa de mi tía*?"[34] I had no idea what he was talking about. He just kept shouting "*mujerzuela!*[35]" through his sniffles until his voice couldn't anymore. With each shout there was a blow to my ribs, left side, and

---

[34] "*Tu coño es tan caliente que mierda en la casa de mi tía*" translates to "Your pussy is so hot that you fucking in my aunt's house."

[35] *Mujerzuela* translates to Slut.

right side from Carlito's fists. I managed to get from under his storm of blows and climb out the window to the fire escape and up to the roof. I grabbed Dino on the way out. I knew his crying and yelling may have gotten him slapped around by Carlito's rage. Running from Carlito I ran into Rhonda and Bowlegged Jackie on the roof. The three of us had concluded that Magdalena had been whispering lies in Carlito's ear. Carlito had time to confront and convict me of fucking somebody but hadn't come around in 2 weeks to see if we were eating. What did he care if I was fucking; wasn't he laid up with his chia Muñeca? I wanted to run and not look back but where would I run? I was a teenager with no money and couldn't speak the language of the land. I was trapped by Carlito's ways. Even in my youthful eyes I was uncomfortable with my whole life arrangement; but hanging with Rhonda and bowlegged Jackie took my mind from my life and gave me a peek into theirs. I was admiring their jeans not only because they had the same name as my oldest son but because I had never owned a pair of jeans. I would trade in all my Dominican styled dresses for just one pair. I would also give up my heels for a pair of their sneakers. I would do anything to be a regular American teenage girl instead of a Dominican wife. An American teenager was free, they picked their own style. My Dominican wife style of dress, living and breathing was a style handed down from generation to the next. My life was the story of many young girls who lose their youth to culture. For the next month and half I was laid up after the conversation with Carlito's fist talking to my ribs. Curandera's prognosis was for me to rest my broken ribs in a painful corset. Magdalena was against Curandera's words and insisted on hospital care but Carlito refused to hear Magdalena's words. For the 1st time in my life I agreed with Curandera. She suggested I stay in bed for the next 2 months. Carlito and the boys were to stay away from me while I healed. And to top it all off I needed an **Enfermera**[36]. The news of Carlito having to pay for someone to care for me made his body jitter and caused his nose to run. Carlito took the boys to his mother's house. The whole 6 weeks I was on bed rest; Carlito nor the boys came to visit me once. For the first 2 weeks I was only on liquids because it was too painful to swallow. On week 3 I finally was able to get up and bathe myself instead of the usual sponge baths. On week 4 Enfermera time was up. Carlito's money had expired. The next 14 days I lived like a **Sistah!**"

---

[36] **Enfermera** translates to nurse.

"Loving with no limit is real love, real love is hard to find but harder to keep."

"I've been in the states for 3 months. I was more than ready to return to DR. After being trapped in the match box called a room and laying in the twin size bed that had formed to my frame for a month, my ribs were still in pain but not excruciating like before. I was able to walk around with Daniel's help. Daniel was feeling guilty for my beating. I did spare him any guilt and promised another round after his help but it didn't stop our blooming friendship. To my surprise Rhonda and Jackie came to visit me. I cried like a baby. Not because I was sad but because Rhonda showed me concern. In my 17 years of life I never had been showed concern. The next 14 days I lived like an American teenager alongside the Sistahs.' Rhonda and bowlegged Jackie recreated me. They dressed me in the skin tight jeans I had admired on them. They traded my Dominican

high heels for a pair of ice white Reebok© two strap fifty four elevens. Rhonda cornrowed my hair. During the day they took me on field trips. The statue of liberty trip was the one that stuck out in my mind. A woman standing alone in the water. She was strong, solid and beautiful. *"**Se puso de pie por la libertad de las mujeres a vivir por la vida no viven de la cultura**"[87]*The statue represented the change of my mind state. They even took me to see a movie. "Parenthood" was a fun experience. I loved just being with the Sistahs! I felt the unconditional love. In the evening if we were at Chyenne's apartment, the original **Pink Pussy Cat**[38], and if we weren't there we

---

[37] ***Se puso de pie por la libertad de las mujeres a vivir por la vida no viven de la cultura*** translates to "She stood for freedom to women to live by life not live by culture."

[38] The ***Pink Pussy Cat*** is Rhonda's production. It's a two bedroom apartment on the upper west side. The apartment is lined with every sexual pleasure known to man. From varieties of sexual creams and oils to dildos. The apartment has scented

were somewhere else partying. Yes it was a time Crystal, Chyenne, Rhonda, Sammy and Tay were all in one place laughing, loving and living life. Most importantly the Sistahs' taught me how to speak English and my way around New York City. I could now be dropped in any of the 5 boroughs and still find my way home. The key to New York City was that all trains had 42ⁿᵈ street in common. I went back in time when all eyes were on me no matter where I went. I showered in the stares. I was feeling amazing I almost forgot about my "floating ribs" being fractured in 7 places, 3 on the right and 4 on the left. Yes the Sistahs' took me to a professional doctor not some old woman with a thousand beads hanging from

---

tea lights posted in various locations to a stripper pole in the living room. From a lip shaped couches to chilled champagne bottles. The living room glass coffee table has a candy dish over flowing with magnum condoms as a center piece to electric chocolate fountain. From a Jacuzzi hot tub in the bathroom surrounded by pink and red butterflies painted on the bathroom walls, to a Chinese spinal Technique Massaging Chair. It's a home away from home to take care of emotional or sexual frustration.

her neck. Curandera holding up on lies and her wooden cane. I missed Dino and wondered if he was being treated right. Ana, Carlito's mother just didn't have the words of a loving grandmother. I planned to go get the boys after my last night of a real American teenage life. On my last night me and the Sistahs 'went to an illegal pit bull dog fight in a basement of a store on 103ʳᵈ street. The fight was ran by Santiago. Santiago was scary looking. He had 'ease by you' eyes that burned the skin. Rhonda's only interest was Kemo's dog, "Killer". The winner of these fights won 100 thousand dollars. For a payout that large guns were part of the outfit. The 6, 5" 337 pounds Big Moose was on the door with a sword of shot guns in both hands. Killer's opponent was Roc's red nose pit bull. Before the fight Roc walked over to us trying to spit game to Tay. Roc's words fell on Tay's deaf ears. He promised if he won, he would buy her attention. We all laughed Roc back to his corner. They ranged the bell to signal the beginning to the dog *fight. Kemo and Roc unleashed their dogs. They fought for their lives. Killer won the fight by sinking his teeth into his neck and held his teeth in place until Roc's dog just gave up fighting and ultimately gave up living. Roc's dog had accepted death and then welcomed it. I wasn't gonna die like that. I wasn't gonna allow Carlito to sink his fists into me until I welcomed death. I had survived my mother's and Curandera's fucked predictions. I could and would beat Carlito. Kemo was filled with joy from his 100 thousand dollar win. From the corner of my eyes I saw two guys in the right wing. Their eyes glued to Kemo's hands handling his winnings. Kemo closed the suitcase and headed for the exit. I trailed behind and watched the two guys with hungry eyes. Rhonda, the other Sistahs' and Jackie climbed into Kemo's SUV. Kemo was having some small talk with his friend. The two guys were going in for the kill. They had already had their guns drawn. I ran up behind Kemo and grabbed his 357 magnum out the back of his waist and started letting loose at the guys with the hungry eyes. I hit one in the shoulder and one in the leg. The kick back from firing the gun hurt my ribs and sprained my right wrist. Kemo hopped in the driver's side of the SUV and I ran around to the right side of the SUV where the Sistahs 'were holding the sliding door open. I loved the rush; it made me feel like I was back in the DR sun with my brothers at my side. I often shot rounds on my brother's farm. The loud sound popped my ears like when I was in the elevator in the empire state building with the Sistahs'. Kemo gave me 10 thousand dollars just for having his back. The money bought me my style, many jeans, many different fifty four elevens and a piece of freedom. With the money I didn't have to depend on Carlito's money. I went to Ana's house and picked up the boys. To my surprise Muñeca was living in Ana's house. At 5 years old Pedro disrespect was full grown. He loved to show off kicking and yelling. Edwin continued to follow in his brother's footsteps. They cried about staying and waiting on their Papi. Ana called to Carlito's store and told him I was stealing the boys. Carlito met me and the boys at Magdalena's apartment. When Carlito set his eyes on the new me, jeans, sneakers and braids, his manhood stood in approval. His lips were filled with sorry's, I love you's and I miss you's. He confessed about his drug addiction and his addiction to the past, Muñeca. My ears took Carlito's apology but my heart didn't accept it. The psychological trauma of Carlito's way to love had my mind twisted. The Carlito my eyes was looking at was the one I hated because it was the Carlito I didn't know. I was looking at the Carlito that held me down and raped me in the same room the boys were sleeping in. The same man that would bruise my body from the neck down. How could his warm words say he loved me but his cold fist swung with fiery? I wanted to know how could he beat the mother of his kids in front of them? How could he make me cry my eyes* out thinking I was doing something wrong? I couldn't relate to my mother but I could understand her. Emotional pain didn't have a cure. The pain hurts to the point of wanting to surrender life but I was stronger than my mother. I wouldn't succumb to the pain. But the words Carlito was speaking at the moment was like a breeze on a humid city summer day. The words soothed my bruises on my skin and refreshed my sight. For the next two weeks I tip toed around Carlito hoping that the he wouldn't turn back to the man I hated. I enjoyed the tenderness of diamonds. I loved the emotion in his gifts. I was not proud of it but I stayed in love with the memory of the Carlito I fell in love with. I tried and tried but couldn't escape the memory. It was like I was living in a dream. He had the power to control my young heart and mind. September was here in no time. I had begun high school at 18 years old. Edwin and Pedro had begun kindergarten at 6 years old. Miguel was in preschool and my baby Dino started going to **Chacha** [39]on the

2nd *floor of Magdalena's building. The Carlito I hated was back in full effect. A Dominican wife didn't need school but I was an aspiring American teenager and school was necessary. I was on call for my Carlito to return. My heart would crawl to my him anytime he appeared. Carlito stopped by once a week to drop off money, a wrist, rib tickle or cum, then he went back to handling "business". I loved school. I inhaled the knowledge like air. I would go to school, after 8 hours of education, I would pick up Edwin and Pedro, then run to the daycare center to get Miguel and then be on my way to the match box room, pick up Dino on the way upstairs and Dino never wanted to walk up, so I had to carry him. I would cook and do my homework at the same time. After dinner, while Dino and Miguel played in the bath tub I would do homework with Edwin and Pedro. Then bathe Edwin and Pedro. Then put all the boys down to sleep and it only took 8 hours to do it. Then at 10 pm I would meet*

---

[39] **Chacha** *translates to baby sitter.*

Rhonda, Jackie and Tay on the roof for our daily joint and laughs. Sometimes all the Sistahs' came. Then I would go to bed and do it all over again the next day, five days a week. On Fridays Carlito would drop in to drop off his weekly loads of trouble. It was a gamble; it was either hits, money or sex. At 6 am Saturday morning Carlito would pick Edwin and Pedro up and take them to the gym that I found out later, he owned. Saturday mornings was my bonding time with Miguel and Dino. We baked, practiced letters and numbers, in English and in Spanish. Sundays I paid Chacha to watch the boys for 5 hours of freedom. I would sleep peacefully for 2 of the hours and chill with the Sistahs' for the last 3 hours. Rhonda, Tay and Crystal hung with the bosses of the street game. I won the respect of the bosses from the incident at the dog fight. On Sunday the bosses took off and girlfriends or chias all hung out. While the girlfriends or chias were off in the corner bragging about what their boss bought them

I was rolling dice with the bosses. Taking their money was like a piece of pie. I could buy any material thing I wanted. Many of the bosses' eyes were on my body rather than watching the dice. Rhonda said I shouldn't see my beauty as a curse but as a gift. My beauty made men adore me and I should enjoy the treasure in their pockets. I caught the eye of 2 men I wished I had never seen. **Caco**[40] *tried to rob and rape me on 103rd street tunnel after a successful dice game that ended at 4 in the morning. I was walking to the nearest ave to catch a cab. Caco didn't know I was prepared but my three fifty seven given as a gift from Kemo made Caco aware. I shot him in his throat. There was so much blood. I looked on all sides of me after backing up against the tunnel's wall to see if anybody was around. Caco breathing down my neck took me to the day Jorge had cornered me. I ran to the nearest ave with the nose of the gun burning the flesh off my right side. I have a plastic-*

---

[40] **Caco** *translates to thief.*

looking patch to remind me of the day. The hot metal was 10 times more painful than Carlito's fists. In the cab my worries were all around Chacha's attitude. I was supposed to had been back hours ago. I calmed Chacha's attitude with money. I had won 5 thousand dollars of street money. Me and the boys made it up the stairs to Magdalena's apartment. My heart dropped to find Carlito sitting on the twin sized mattress. I was amazed he didn't jump on me but instead needed my presence. His citizenship had been approved and my signature was needed to get Carlito's father's money. After being in America for 6 months we were finally going to get the money. Me and the boys moved from the match box to a house in the south Bronx. The Sistahs' stayed true to their word and came to visit me. I would still chill with them when I got the chance. Carlito promised to live as a family but instead nothing changed. He was gone 5 days out of the week and home on Saturdays. He would return after the Saturday morning gym training with the boys and forced himself on me. Sunday usually was when the Sistahs' came to visit me at the house. The second problem that came from the dice game was the eyes of Hugo. I felt the magic, and wanted to breathe the mysteries in the air between us. We walked down to lover's lane without giving in the love we shared in our eyes. Being with Hugo made me reminisce on the days in DR when there was love in my mother's heart and in my father's eyes. Being with Hugo filled me with the emotion of being the average teenager with a crush. I was in a pleasant mood all the time and nothing could break me floating on a cloud. I begged Chacha in advance to watch the boys so I could attend the 1990 New Year's Eve party. That party was the beginning of become Brooklyn Zoo and the end of Carlito's Dominican wife. "

"The breakthrough of Nineteen ninety the place and a year to remember."

"*1990 was a year to remember but if you didn't notice, in my life I gotta go through the bad to get to the good. Mercedes had moved in with me and the boys. Let me tell how that happened. I would never volunteer to share my space with Mercedes. My father had the time and resources to find Carlito and asked him if Mercedes could stay with "us" for a while, her mother was going through some hard times. It amazed me how my father was seeking help for Mercedes 'cus her mother was going through some hard times. I went through many hard time where were you for me, Papi? I waited for my father to save me from my mother? But "us" didn't included Carlito. My father should have asked me but nonetheless I returned home to Mercedes sitting on the front steps to my house. Okay, let me rewind to how my day went prior to being greeted by*

Mercedes's bags and all on my front step. I'm telling you, it's some things that just can't be made up. First thing in the morning the boiler was acting weird, the water would be cold longer then it was hot. The boys had taken their baths last night. I was just too worn out last night to eat or shower. Pedro made everything a chore. I chased him to eat. I chased him to color the shapes. His rebellious soul made him break every crayon in half. I didn't trust the boy with scissors in his hand so I cut the shapes my damn self. The glue was off limits for Pedro, too. I put one dot of glue on the spot where the shapes went. You think he could handle putting the shapes down on the paper like any normal 5 year old but I had to guide his playful hand. A few hours with Pedro felt like a 9 to 5 overworked, under paid job. And Edwin's laughter of encouragement in the background didn't help. Try cooking and doing homework on top of all of that. Afterwards, I got them settled in their rooms. Edwin and Dino shared a room. With Pedro out of the picture,

Edwin was very helpful. He would lay holding Dino's little body. Pedro and Miguel shared a room. Miguel would pretend to help clean up the food that was intentionally thrown on the wooden floor by that boy Pedro. Thanks to living at Magdalena's apartment having to rent plates, I only believed in paper plates. Miguel was waiting for Pedro to go to sleep before going to bed. At 4 years old Miguel was very smart. He could read two letter words and he was only in preschool. After Miguel fell asleep I would just fall out in my house sweats and tee shirt. I woke up late and the boiler was doing the weird thing to the water temperature. I ran to the kitchen and scrambled some eggs for the boys. And boiled water to take a birdbath. After that I sat Edwin and Pedro down at their kiddie table to eat. Edwin had on t-shirt, jeans, socks and sneakers, like he was supposed too. Pedro had on t-shirt and jeans, no socks and no sneakers. I couldn't begin to start a fight with his little ass. I dressed and fed Miguel and Dino at the same time. I went to check up on Edwin and Pedro. Edwin had his school shirt, coat, hat and book bag on. Pedro had on his t-shirt, jeans, one sock, one sneaker and a grin on his face. I went to get dressed, I dared Pedro not to be ready when I came back. I didn't believe in hitting the boys but Pedro could push a person to homicide or even suicide. Carlito had built a high tolerance of pain in the boys. Beating Pedro's ass had no effect on his behavior. I had to make it to school today. Today was the last day of class before the winter break of 6 days, 8 days with Saturday and Sunday included, for Christmas and New Year's. Carlito wanted to have a Christmas party at MY house in the Bronx. I wanted something small with just me and the boys. An American Christmas, with a tree and gifts was my idea but wasn't even heard by Carlito's ears. It was his way in his house. He joked and said after the party it was going to take me a few days to clean the house spotless, he'd take the boys so I could do a proper job. Joke was on him I *had already recruited the Sistahs' to help, so I could have days to actually hang out with my friends like a real teenager. First, I dropped Edwin and Pedro off to their public school 4 blocks away from the house. I kissed them both on the cheek at the school door, of course Pedro wiped my kiss off. I heard somebody yelling "Ms. Cruz". The yell was getting closer, so I turned around. It was a woman out of breath. She caught her breath and then explained who she was. Her daughter was in the class with Pedro and her daughter was afraid of him. I wanted to say "shit, me too". Pedro threatened to cut the girl's hair off. I apologized and told her I would talk to him. The woman went crazy and started screaming about young bitches having babies and couldn't raise them. She went on and on. I had listened for too long and my fist started talking for me. One square hit to the bridge of her nose and blood squirted out like a shaken up can soda, right on to my coat. I had to run back home and change while shifting Dino from hip to hip* and hustling Miguel to walk faster. I finally got Miguel to preschool, Dino to Chacha and myself to school, in 8 degree weather. After school I had a 2 hour window where I hung with the Sistahs! They usually grouped up and then came to pick me up from school. Tay was hardly around these days. She was a waitress at "Sweet Cheeks". We say strip club Tay say bar and she was sleeping with Christopher, the married owner. After school the Sistahs' showed up as promised. Rhonda had Kemo wrapped around her finger. I loved to watch her have power and control over him. The view was something forbidden on Dominican soil. You know, Rhonda had Kemo chauffeur her around. As soon as I got in the car Kemo passed me a joint and good news. Smoking marijuana was the medicine to my internal pain of life. From the Sistahs' I learned that American label, Domestic Violence, which was the way of Carlito's love. Speaking to the Sistah's ears of how Carlito loved me would have made it reality to me. Even though I was living a nightmare I *dreamed it wasn't true. Plus I didn't want to see my shame and blame in the Sistahs' eyes. The Sistahs' surprised me with a beeper just like they all had. With the beeper I had no excuse of missing the New Year's Eve party that was in a week. After becoming an average American teenager with a beeper, I just chilled with the Sistahs' for the next hour and a half. I had to go back to being a Dominican house wife, even though I didn't want to, I knew I had to. Being with the Sistahs' was a change in pace. Nobody calling out "Mama", nobody crying and no fights. I loved being with them. They loved me for me and I loved them right back. So, Edwin and Pedro were the 1st stop. Of course when picking up Pedro, you also picked up an ear full of his classroom behavior. Well today it wasn't the teacher, Ms. Winnie, giving the report it was police officers. They were explaining to me that Pedro had snapped the neck of the classroom pet hamster. It was a criminal act but because of his age he was required to seek* counseling. The officer's words had me speechless. How could a 5 year old be a killer? Yes I wanted to beat Pedro ass from the fight I got into this morning thanks to his threats; but beating his ass became an everyday affair with no results, he hardly cried. I was thinking up a punishment on my way to pick up Miguel. My mind hadn't come up with anything yet, I contemplated some more on the way to pick up Dino. My mind skipped passed Pedro and was focused on the Christmas and New Year's Eve party with the bosses. Not only was it a money opportunity it was also a chance for my eyes to soak up Hugo. While I was gathering Dino's belongs I reminded Chacha about the parties. Today was Friday, and Sunday night I had to cook for the Christmas Eve party for Carlito's family. Carlito's plan was to put on a performance of a loving family, with me and the boys. On my way home I ran into Daniel. Daniel's clothes were filthy. He had clumps of dirt caked up in his hair. He looked like a dirt bomb went off in his hands. But the look of abandonment, broken heartedness and lost soul in Daniel's eyes spoke to my heart. I needed and wanted to help him. Magdalena had put Daniel and Steven out. Steven had surrendered his soul and pockets to crack. And ya know Magdalena's rules: no money, no home. Daniel had been living on the streets of Washington heights for weeks. I had only been outta Magdalena's house for just 3 weeks and so much had changed. I gave Daniel the key to the basement of my house and the address. He could come and go as he pleased. Carlito was barely home and when he was, he would never go to the basement. It wasn't much but it was safe. I handed him a few dollars and headed home, to find Mercedes's ass sitting on the step of my house. I hadn't seen her since I was 8 years old. I was kinda happy to see her because looking at her face was looking into my past life before the curse. Her body hadn't adjusted to New York's winter cold air. Her teeth were chattering. I opened the *front door to let Mercedes and the boys into the warmth of my house. It was odd that the house was a home without Carlito. With Carlito inside it was house of bricks and wood. Yeah, my thoughts too… now the boiler WAS working. I sat the boys down in the living room in front of the television with snacks. Due to the season Charlie brown was on rotation and their attention was caught. With their attention being held I could start cooking. On Fridays I made pasta dishes to last for two nights 'cus ya girl didn't cook on Saturdays. So I started chopping up my peppers, a piece of garlic and fresh oregano. My ears paid attention to the worded update of Mercedes's life to the present. Mercedes was sent to New York by her mother due to Mercedes's lies of being "PURE"; she was exposed. In DR Mercedes's tinted purity would land her an average farm worker. Men of DR's high stature married for the purity and nothing else. I guess I kinda get it, to have something nobody will ever get is a priceless gift. Meanwhile my mind was* focused on what could happen at either party. There was always action at these parties. People didn't only wear their best but they were dipped in love, hate or looking for a date. All three can result into a fight. Saturday I cleaned the two story 4 bedroom house from ceiling to windows down to the floors. Mercedes kept an eye on the boys while I cleaned and cooked. Daniel knocked on the kitchen floor from the basement to tell me he was hungry. I took food down to him. While I was down in the basement I did the laundry and talked to Daniel. He looked clean and healthy after a plate of home cooked food and a place to rest his head. Daniel started to look like himself. Sunday morning the house was woken up by Carlito's return. He had a box of glass plates. I am a paper plate type of girl but Carlito wouldn't have his family eating off paper plates. It had been about 10 days since I last saw Carlito. His skin had aged in the 6 months by years. It was the drugs wearing down his skin and today he was looking elderly. I started cooking early in the morning. I didn't want Carlito's family to start showing up before dinner was ready. Last night I made the **ensalada de papa**[41], **pernil**[42], **bizcocho de mantequilla con cobertura de chocolate pastel de mantequilla con cobertura de chocolate**[43] and a small Flan. All I had left to make was **arroz y frijoles**[44] **and tostones**[45]. Since Mercedes was here I put her ass to work. I got started on the arroz y frijoles while she began to peel the 50 plátanos[46].The food was done before Carlito's family started to arrive. Me and the boys had showered and dressed. To avoid problems I transformed back into the Dominican house wife uniform. In fact I

---

[41] **ensalada de papa** translates to potato salad

[42] **Pernil** translates to pork

[43] **bizcocho de mantequilla con cobertura de chocolate pastel de mantequilla con cobertura de chocolate** translates to butter cake with chocolate frosting.

[44] **arroz y frijoles** translates to rice and beans.

[45] **Tostones** translates to thin sliced plantains fried

[46] **Plátanos** translates to plantains, green bananas

wore the same red sequenced dress that I met Rhonda in on Magdalena's building rooftop. Carlito amazingly had enough money to fly his family members in to celebrate our 1st Christmas in America. I was kinda grateful that Mercedes was here. I was always in Carlito's family company and felt like an outsider. They made sure to make me feel like "Carlito's wife" was my only identity. The party was somewhat pleasant until Carlito's mother felt the need to bring up Muñeca. I was running around serving 21 people food and drinks, that didn't include my boys. My feet were sore and my back was hurting. But with filled bellies they disrespected me and my house by speaking of Carlito's chia's name. Out the side of my eye I saw Carlito and Mercedes talking too close for comfort. I was doing too much and too much was going on for me to confront Mercedes. Then Pedro pulled down the six foot Christmas tree, fully dressed with blinking lights, glass hand painted ornaments and garland. My right eye started twitching. I needed everybody to get the fuck out. Carlito was big spending; he had put his family up in a hotel. Me and the boys lived in the house 24 days by ourselves. Carlito had been by 2 times with $500; it helped but I still had to dip into my dice winnings to feed and clothe all 4 of us. With everybody gone and a sink, counter and table all crammed with dirty plates, cups, pots and pans, Carlito stayed true to his words and took the boys with him when the party was over. I had four days to live and I did. The next morning me and Mercedes started cleaning before the Sistahs' arrived one by one. We had the house spotless by 3pm on Christmas afternoon. Me and the Sistahs' were all excited to be going to the bosses of all bosses Christmas party later that night. I had invited Mercedes outta pure courtesy, but was happy when she declined. For the next 6 hours I lounged around, ate and took a nap. I was prepping by 9. The party didn't start until 11 but I had to look good. I had eyes for Hugo. My eyes were so on him that I didn't even bother checking Mercedes for flirting with Carlito. When the Sistahs' went out they dressed as a unit. We all had on white buttoned fly levi jeans, a pair of fifty four elevens in 6 different flavors and matching tee shirts. The Sistahs' had a hook up with EJ, he spray painted our names on the tee shirt in graffiti writing. I thought it was cool to have my name written like the subway graffiti. The DJ S and S spun records from hammer to the fresh prince. Rhonda taught me how to shake my ass to uncle Luke's voice. I found out I was living in the boogie down. I listened to the words of the public enemy fighting for the power. The music was just like the time of nice and smooth sway to life. It was the time to be in New York City. The LL lip licking could get you to 3rd base. I fell in love with EPMD unfinished business. Oddly enough that's how I viewed the boys as unfinished business from DR. I waited all night to see if Hugo would show. I ended the dice game at 3 am. I walked away with almost 100 *thousand dollars. And no, I wasn't scared not even a little. I always packed the heat of a gun. Hugo always joked I was a henny colored pit bull with a killer body and killer bite. As we were exiting the house party, basically it was a crack head home take over. Rhonda opened the project elevator door and Hugo was standing right there. "Aww, yall leaving already? Killer, I know you left some money in dem niccas pockets for me?" Hugo words made me blush. The Sistahs' noticed it and playfully teased me about it. The Sistahs' came back to my house. We stood up all night recapping the events that took place at the party. Who came with who? and Who left with somebody different than the person they came with? Who had on what? And Who had on somebody else's clothes. Mercedes came downstairs to complain about the noise. We laughed her ass back upstairs. Me and the Sistahs' fell asleep in the living room after eating the leftovers of Carlito's family Christmas eve dinner. We started planning* *our outfits for next week's new year's eve party. We settled on jean suits and we were going to get EJ to spray paint our names on the back of the jean jackets. Time flew, one day I was chilling with the Sistahs' drinking and smoking, and then the next thing it was Friday. Friday afternoon Carlito dropped off EPMD. Miguel had a black eye. I immediately questioned Carlito. His explanation was Pedro and Miguel were fighting over a toy. So Carlito gloved them up and had them go 3 rounds. Pedro obviously won. "**que mi hijo el campeón**[47]" I hated when Carlito made the EPMD fight each other. Surprisingly Carlito stayed at the house for the weekend. I spent Saturday avoiding him. If he went into a room, I went into another. It had been 16 days since I had sex and I didn't intend on having sex with him today. Sunday morning I cooked breakfast. Right after breakfast I finished up the homework packet with Edwin and Pedro. As Pedro disregarded*

---

[47] **que mi hijo el campeón** translates to "My son the champion."

*my words of direction, Carlito had words of encouragement for Pedro's disrespectful behavior. They were "**Hombre de su propia mente, el campeón**"[48] I was getting the EPMD ready to go to Chacha's house after their homework was done. Mercedes again declined going to the New year's eve party. Carlito followed me and the EPMD out the front door. Carlito was talking extra shit 'cus he was mad I was going out. Damn I was trapped with the EMPD all the time could I have a little fun? Yup you guessed it, he called me all kinds of whores and sluts. I ignored Carlito's cocaine sniffles and words. At Chacha's house it was quiet. Chacha was an older dominican woman who enjoyed the company of children. She would always say I was helping her more than she was helping me. We gave Chacha a gift bag of slippers and house coats, with the pockets just the way she liked it, as a Christmas present. I ran some errands for Chacha and enjoyed*

---

[48] ***hombre de su propia mente, el campeón*** translates to *"A man of his own mind, the champion."*

receiving parental advice before I was ready to leave. It was around 6 pm when I left Chacha's house. I couldn't wait to get to the legendary building 1990 new year's eve party. There was no dice game and everybody was drinking heavy. The evening's entertainment began early with Rhonda and Chyenne's small argument. Rhonda was voicing her opinion of Ace, Chyenne's shadow attending all "Sistah only" events. Sammy, the peace maker ended the word shouting match. At some point me and Hugo were on the sideline talking. Nothing could've been sweeter than the sound of making love with words. Nothing was forbidden; we shared every detail of our life. I found out that Hugo had a 10 year old son. A son he was raising by himself. The mother of his son was a victim of crack. He did 5 years in jail for hustling. He still had money in the game, he just wasn't a player. He was 32 years old. He couldn't believe I was just 18 with the life I had lived. He concluded I was a strong woman and would become stronger with every tear. If only I just had one person to be there for me with advice of wisdom, like Hugo gave I would be just fine. I would've given the world to make him mine. He had grace, style and thug in his words. He was everything Carlito wasn't. Carlito had changed into a drug fueled monster. The party ended after the ball dropped, people were locking lips. And I had to return home to get some sleep and pick up EPMD from Chacha by noon. School was back in full effect the next day. As me and the Sistahs' parted ways, Chyenne hit us with the bomb... she was pregnant. We all handed her congratulations kisses and hugs. I entered the house. I could smell sex in the air. I went up to my bed room where my ears were following the moans. My eyes would've like to fall outta my head. It was Carlito fucking the shit outta Mercedes. Of course I beat Mercedes's ass. I pistol whipped her. The hits weren't only for having sex with Carlito, they were also because Papi called my house to speak to her. I envied the relationship she shared with Papi. Mercedes ended up with two black eyes, a broken nose and broken cheek bone. I beat her ass solely off of Papi principle, I could've cared less about Carlito. Carlito's mouth shot out a bunch of sorry's but they only came because of the gun in my hand. Carlito's main concern was that Muñeca didn't find out about his infidelity. At that very moment I realized just what I was to Carlito. I was just something he needed to get what and who he wanted. To be used, hurt but to be used by someone you love and trust, the pain is 10 times worst. I put Mercedes and her shit out on my front steps. Carlito ran out the door right after I put Mercedes out. I never seen it before but I could see the fear in Carlito's bright cocaine eyes. He stayed away from the house for the next month and a half. He returned to the house on me and Dino's birthday. The day after America's Valentine's day. Carlito was trying to be all nice but it felt phony. When Daniel banged on the floor, my eyes widened. I wanted to run upstairs and grab a gun from under my pillow. Just my luck; Carlito heard the bang and wanted to go down to check it out. I tried to keep him from going down in the basement. The more I tried to keep him from the basement the more he wanted to go. I caved in and told him to go downstairs while I go upstairs. My suggestion wasn't an option. Carlito dragged me across the floor by my hair. I begged Carlito to stop his madness. EPMD also begged. Carlito's ears stopped working properly a long time ago. Carlito wrapped his boxer bear paws around my neck to bring me to my feet and made me lead the way down into the basement. He said whatever was down there would get me first. All hell broke loose when Carlito spotted movement. He unhanded my neck and investigated with a flash light. He found Daniel hiding in behind the dryer. I was creeping up the stairs. I needed to get to my room. I had to move slow so the wooden stairs wouldn't squeak. Carlito looked around a little with his flashlight and quickly discovered that Daniel was living in the basement. I had 4 more stairs to be able to run for my gun. Carlito dragged me down to the basement stairs. It happened so fast. I didn't even hear him coming. I yelled out. EPMD came to the landing, their little hearts cried out to me but Carlito slammed the door to the basement in EPMD's face. I could hear their little voices **"La dejó ir!"**[49] And little fists banging on the door. **"No se puede tener el coño que me pertenece, pero el culo es todo tuyo"**[50]. As Carlito announced his intentions he was taking off his clothes and told Daniel to do the same. I cried and begged Carlito to let me take a shower. I said everything under the sun to get up stairs. Carlito ripped my clothes off; I gave a little struggle. Carlito cooled down my fight when he pulled out his 357. Carlito made up the story that I was fucking Daniel since Magdalena's apartment. How

---

[49] **la dejó ir** translates to "Let her go."
[50] **no se puede tener el coño que me pertenece, pero el culo es todo tuyo** translates to "You can't have the pussy that belongs to me but the ass is all yours."

dare I betray him by bringing him to his house? Carlito shouted about my beauty was for him and since I insisted on sharing it with Daniel I was going to share it in front of him. The jealousy in his eyes was eyes I never seen. I screamed, cried and begged Carlito to stop. But the look in his eyes was the stares of the devil. He threw me on the floor. He roughly entered me. As he had sex with me his breath steaming down on the side of my skin. His strokes were like lashes for his resentment toward my betrayal. His cocaine dripped from his nose onto my face. I hadn't had sex in 2 months. The pain of being touched was nothing compared to the violation and humiliation that had come with Carlito's unwanted touch. Next, it was Daniel's turn. Daniel didn't want to take advantage of me but with Carlito's cocaine hand holding a gun to his head, literally, changed his mind. Daniel did as he was told. Carlito directed Daniel's movements inside my asshole like a movie director, as he inhaled large amounts of cocaine. "lift the leg up", "Get in that ass" and "**duro**"[51] Carlito shouted as he took breaks to fill his nose with sniffs of power. I heard the flesh of my asshole rip open. I cried out in excruciation, torturous pain that was given stab by stab from Daniel. Each brutal stab ripped another inch of my flesh. Daniel had tears of emotional pain. Carlito threw Daniel out after they both were finished. Carlito called Daniel all types of homosexual insults for crying. Carlito then left with EPMD. I laid in the same spot for the next 24 days, not because I wanted to but because my asshole was completely ripped open, just moving my legs was great pain. Daniel hid in the bushes and waited until Carlito left with EPMD and returned to the scene of the crime. Daniel stood right by my side. He cleaned my ripped asshole of blood and shit. He treated my torn flesh. I was degraded by having to wear diapers. Daniel fed me. It was hard to see the up because I was broken down. The physical injuries were

---

[51] **Duro** translates to harder.

severe but the shot to my heart was fatal to my locked heart for Carlito. Daniel never once looked me in the eyes. I know guilt consumed his thought but my deformed flesh and afflicted heart was in too much agony to console him. Don't get me wrong I owe my life to Daniel. He was there for me when I was in a very dark place and to finally have somebody in my corner was a feeling I hadn't had for years. I always wondered what that felt like. Thanks to Daniel I had something I wished for but never had. The night in the basement haunted Daniel's memory to the point he killed himself years later. I used to blame myself for Daniel's death for years until I realized that Carlito was accountable for Daniel's death. As soon as I was able to walk I ran to the Sistahs'. I wanted to tell them what Carlito did and made Daniel do to me but the shame kept my lips closed. I laid up with Crystal at a hotel room that was owned by one of her mother's former lovers. Crystal was paid a thousand dollars to house sit. Crystal's movements were entertaining. She had invited her secret lover, Kamal Campbell to the hotel room and forgot about the "other guy" she had also invited over. The front desk had called to tell that the "other guy" was here. Crystal left me in the room with Kamal while she got rid of the "other guy". Kamal revealed his ties and commitment to Crystal. Crystal was Kamal's 1st love. Kamal was different. He could hang out but he was also about school. He went to college upstate New York, but came down to hang out with his childhood friends. He would also pick up drugs for his college friends and charge them 4 times the price he paid. Kamal would purchase the drugs from Ace. Ace and Kamal grew up together. Their lives grew in different directions but they remained distant friends. Now they were business partners. Ace would sometime save Kamal the trip and bring drugs to him. Kamal was saving his profit to eventually run away with his secret lover, Crystal. Meanwhile Crystal *was sucking, fucking and pick pocketing the "other guy" in the exit. After Crystal drained the "other guy's" penis and pockets she returned to the room like nothing happened. Years later, I was surprised to find out that the "other guy" was Ace. I could chill around with a smile on my face when it was outta place. Then I got a beep from Hugo. I ran to him. I knew I could tell him about what had happen between me, Carlito and Daniel. I cried my heart out along with the story on to Hugo's ears and chest. Hugo was the sun after the storm. I wanted to kill Carlito right before he begged for his life. But Hugo said death is the easy way out and I should hit a man where it hurts, in his pockets and his bitch. My 1st stop was Marquez's office on 161st street in the Bronx. Carlito didn't make moves without Marquez's approval. Marquez's lips were for sale. For 20 thousand dollars and two 9 millimeters pointed at his face, had bought me all the information I could use against Carlito. We had been in America for 9 months and*

Carlito was very busy. Carlito changed the names on his father's money to EPMD. Carlito had a mini mansion in New Jersey. Carlito owned a gym, a pawn shop and a construction company ran by a Jamaican shotta, Spragga. Spragga had built plenty of buildings on top of dead bodies of people who got in Carlito's way. Carlito had 5 bodegas. Each were selling weights of cocaine to local bosses. Marquez gave up the address dates and times when inventory would be restocked. Carlito also got paid off Santiago's dog fights because Santiago used the basement of Carlito's stores. Carlito had moved Muñeca to a condo in downtown Manhattan and moved Mercedes in his mother's house. Muñeca was given a luxurious life downtown while I was provided the bare necessities uptown. Mercedes was pregnant by Carlito. Marquez told me everything. I carried the information from Marquez to Hugo. Hugo confirmed Marquez's words by watching Carlito's every move for the next month. I went back to my house in the Bronx but couldn't sleep. My mind was set on revenge. Carlito dropped off EPMD without getting out of the car. My hand was shaking to fill his car door with bullets from my guns. I was to go back to my life with EPMD and the Sistahs' and when the time was right we was gonna get Carlito. I wired money to Bryan and Ryan to buy identities so they could come to New York. I had pre-paid their hotel stay and everything. Three men and a woman robbed over 2 million dollars from all of Carlito's spots, drug and dog fight money. Only 2 people chose to sacrifice their lives for Carlito's money. **"La muerte viene de a tres como los estornudos"[52]** When we robbed the pawn shop, Magdalena was running the counter. The sight of the gun gave her an instant fatal heart attack. It all worked for the best I wanted to kill Magdalena for telling Carlito lies about me and Daniel. Her lies cost Daniel his life. I don't shoot kids or the elderly so

---

[52]**La muerte viene de a tres como los estornudos** translates to "Death comes in threes just like sneezes."

Magdalena's heart attack worked out in my favor and I didn't have to endure her blood on my hands. It took Carlito some time but he recovered from the loss of the money. I met Muñeca downtown manhattan at the door of her condo apartment. When her eyes locked with mine, she instantly knew who I was. She was so arrogant. She invited me inside the apartment. She bragged and boosted about all that Carlito had bought and done for her. She understood why I was mad but she insisted that she was here first. I never said a word, I just pulled out the two 9 millimeters. I let Muñeca beg for her life before I shot her between the eyes, Carlito would never recover from this lost. I shot Muñeca not only because it would break Carlito's heart but because she was provided with a luxurious life downtown, when I had to fight for the bare necessities. I approached Spragga with an amount of money he couldn't refuse to give Muñeca a cement nap. We spilt the money evenly between the four of us. Bryan and Ryan went back home richer than when they come. Hugo schooled me to street game to exchange the stolen drugs for money. Hugo's teaching were words I lived by. Hugo had been in the game for years. The game made him a bloodcurdling animal but when we were alone he was gentle as a church mouse. I've seen Hugo make top dogs fall to their knees begging for one more chance. And in the same day Hugo's tender words held me like a new born baby. After all the drugs were sold, Hugo moved to Miami. Hugo leaving, broke my heart I wanted to be with him. The night before he left I gave myself to him. I hadn't been with nobody but Carlito. And what happened with Daniel I didn't consider as sex. Hugo caressed my mind as well as my skin. He fed my hunger to acceptance and love. He took his time, it wasn't rushed like with Carlito. He was concerned with me receiving the pleasure and taking the pleasure like Carlito had. Being under Hugo as his passionate breathing blew across my face took me back home. For one quick minute I was on DR's beach with the clear air in my nose and safe sand under my back. I was prepared to leave everything behind to follow Hugo to the end of the earth. The feeling of just being safe was a feeling I almost forgot about since I didn't have it for so long. He told me the time wasn't now. So I hid my money at Chacha's house until I could think of somewhere else to put it. Carlito came back to my house in the Bronx, begging to live in the basement. The cocaine had completely take over his brain. He was paranoid, sweating and sniffing. I laughed in his face. How the mighty had fallen, but I did let him stay. Having Carlito in the house was like having Ninera again. I still did my motherly duties and then dropped EPMD right off at the house to be watched by Carlito. Carlito cried every night over Muñeca. It gave me great pleasure to see Carlito heart cry out. I knew it was wrong to thrive off the pain of someone else but to see Carlito broke and his heart afflicted by love was music to my soul. EPMD was sent on a *summer vacation with my brothers in DR. I spent that summer with the Sistahs'. I even went to Miami to see Hugo. It was a secret trip I didn't even tell the Sistahs' about it. I had to look in Hugo's eyes, it was my safe haven. I still wanted him til' this day. He still said I wasn't ready. As soon as it was time to go back to school Chyenne gave birth to Polo. Any chance I got I was hanging over little Polo. In no time Thanksgiving was here. I usually cooked up a storm but this year I was house hopping with the Sistahs'. Mercedes gave birth to Carlito's daughter. EPMD said she went in labor at the dinner table. For Christmas I took EPMD to meet Silvia in DR. Silvia was the 1st person to show me love after the curse. Silvia gave the love my mother had lost. Since we were in DR we attended Joanny's wedding. In DR it was like the hands of time had reversed and Carlito's eyes had love in them but as soon as we returned home, in New York, we were back to me hating him and him being mad he didn't have Muñeca. 1990 came to a close* and I had my identity; I was an survivor. I had accepted what I had been through, it made me the woman I was becoming. I had survived Curandera's cruse, my mother's physical torture and Carlito's mental, physical and sexual beatings. I would not allow anyone else to ever abuse me again and if they tried they would catch my bullets. On my 19th birthday, February 15th 1991, Carlito had forbidden me from going out. He said I couldn't leave without cooking a home cooked meal for him and his sons. He insisted that his sons should be eating a home cooked meal and not dinner from a can. The argument started with the can of spaghetti and moved into Chacha's house being off limits. He then went into a rave about me being all types of hoes and an unfit mother. His mouth didn't stop there. He thought that I shouldn't be out party leaving him in pain. He was in agony because Muñeca was missing. He had the balls to want me to console him because his chia was fucking missing. I had heard enough and the Sistahs' just beeped me letting me know they were ready. I put my 9 millimeter on the table before I began talking. I told him I would feed them whatever I wanted and if he didn't like it he could cook whatever he liked. I also calmly told him that since Chacha's house was unsuitable for him, he could watch his own sons. He stood up and I advised him to have a seat. I confessed that I definitely had target practice on his precious Muñeca and if he didn't wanna join her in the spiritual world then he should just relax. His eyes widened. He couldn't believe the words that were coming out of my mouth. He dared me to repeat myself. I told him Muñeca was gone and never coming back. I looked down at my 9 millimeter and then back at Carlito's eyes. I told him he could join his precious Muñeca. The words was a shot to Carlito's heart without breaking the skin. Carlito fought back by throwing a can of spaghetti at me, hitting and shattering my jaw bone. I woke up in Metropolitan hospital's emergency room. I should've killed

Carlito that night. The pain from my jaw replacement and plastic surgery was equivalent to 3 beat downs from Carlito's over sized boxing fist and giving birth 2 times. Could you believe they only gave him 3 years in jail for breaking my jaw? Marquez's snake ass got Carlito out of being deported. For the next six months I was in and out the hospital. Walking around with my face the size of a thanksgiving parade balloon, drinking meals out of a straw. The pain was so bad I would wish to die but anger kept me alive. The Sistahs' jumped right into step. They all took turns taking care of EPMD while I recovered. I was assigned a small beautiful woman from India, her name was Rupashi, it meant beautiful. She told me her journey in her culture with the mark of beauty. I felt the connection between our spirits. Rupashi was a Sistah. Me and Rupashi were born thousands of miles apart and years apart and were born into different cultures with the same circumstances that had bound us. Her skin was coated with the *same Hennessey color just like mine. She cared for me like a mother would her 1st born. 10 days before the wires and the bandages were going to be removed, Rupashi told me a story about a white elephant that changed me. In her culture elephants were warriors, in fact she called them God of warriors. There was one white female elephant born. Female elephants are born with short trunks and no tusk but this female white elephant was born with a trunk and a tusk. The female white elephant trunk grew longer than the male elephants and the tusk grew bigger and stronger than any male elephant the owner had ever trained. The owner trained the white elephant like he had trained elephants before. But when it was time for war the owner decided the white elephant was too beautiful to fight even though the white female elephant was the strongest of the herd. The female white elephant was given to a town. The elephant was no longer of value to the owner. The town loved and cared for the white elephant* as a community. They put color bangles on her tusk. Each color had a meaning. "New beginnings, of happiness, independence, luck and success" were the white, yellow, purple, green, and orange bangles. "The change of energy due to wisdom" were the red and blue bangles. "The power is in strength, and strength is fortune" were the black, sliver and white gold bangles. As Rupashi told the story she laid out the bangles. The town was attacked. The female white elephant never forgot her warrior training and saved the town. I was the white elephant carrying the weight of 130 people. I was unable to speak. How did she know I needed that story at that time? When the bandages and wires were removed, I went looking for Rupashi so I could thank her. I searched and never found a clue. I was given public assistance, public housing and counseling for being a victim of domestic violence. In DR, all that Carlito had done to me was viewed as normal life as a Dominican wife but in America this treatment made me a victim.

Carlito made me a statistic, I was the 1 of every 4 woman who had been intimidated, physically, mentally and sexually assaulted, battered deeper than skin, by their husband. A man you once trusted with your life has turned your love into mistrust and to have your life in the hands of a man you don't trust was a the scariest ride of a lifetime. Carlito's abuse had created a monster in Pedro. Pedro had channeled what Carlito did to me into his own behavior to his wife. The next three years I began to heal. I started to love me. And by loving me I was able begin to love EPMD. It was very hard to look at EPMD and see their little faces. When I looked at them I saw Carlito. I became a woman at 22 years old with Edwin and Pedro 10 years old, Miguel 9 years old and Dino 8. "

"No more drama is the production of life in Harlem"

Brooklyn was given her street clothes. She began to dress in symbols of her journey. She first unraveled her cornrows. Brooklyn's free flowing jet black hair was one of the pleasant reminders of her mother before her mother lost the mental battle to love. Brooklyn's mother's hair flowed down to her feet but after the break up with Brooklyn's father she cut all her hair off. She slipped on her black India tunic dress. She wears indian clothes in honor of Rupashi. She puts liquid concealer on the less than half an inch scar under her right jaw line from the surgeries. Last but not least she puts on her gold bangles; the mark of the white elephant on her wrist and she puts on her signature gold chandelier earrings. She is released from the back doors of the criminal court building on 100 Center Street. The Sistahs', Rhonda and Sammy are there to embrace Brooklyn. Brooklyn was in jail for 73 days and hadn't shed one tear until now. She was sobbing on Rhonda's shoulder as Sammy wrapped her arms around Brooklyn and Rhonda. Brooklyn is shedding tears for the little girl in DR that was beaten by her mother. She weeps for her innocence that was taken by Carlito. Some of the tears in her eyes are tears of joy. Joy for the woman she has become with the odds and world against her. Brooklyn pulls her head up from the huddle.

"I'm starving! I need real food" Brooklyn announces

"UNCLE TITI'S" the three Sistahs' shout in unison.

Uncle Titi's is a local diner in Morningside Heights. The theme of the diner is the fifties era. The waitresses all wear a light pink fifties signature "poodle-skirt", embellished with a huge, fuzzy chenille French poodle, riding over a cloud of stiff, bouffant petticoats. Staying true to the theme of the diner, the waitress feet are covered in the original fifties black and white saddle shoes. *Uncle Titi's* is a restaurant owned by Marc and Mildred, a mother and son team. The sister and nephew of Tay. Marc and Mildred share many feminine ways but cooking is the only trait of Marc, Mildred takes pride in. *Uncle Titi's* served southern soulful breakfast, lunch and dinner. The Sistahs' had already picked up Brooklyn's Maybach 62 S, 2011 model, for her. Rhonda handed Brooklyn the keys to her car.

"I don't really wanna give her back." Rhonda joked with Brooklyn through her laugher.

"You was sporting my car?" Brooklyn questions.

"Just a little. She rides smooth and never mind the attention she attracts." Rhonda confesses her enjoyment in Brooklyn's car.

Marc and Mildred greet the Sistah's when they entered the diner with hugs and kisses as they were seated at a table.

"You gotta start from the beginning, what the fuck happened?" Rhonda questions Brooklyn

"I only went to Crystal's house to convince her to drop the charges against Chyenne. Chyenne is pregnant was my gonna be my plea but when I got there Kamal was lacing the house with gasoline."

"He never got over Crystal?" Sammy inquired

"I think he's been over Crystal. It's the hurt that he's wasn't over. Crystal fed him lies. Crystal and Kamal had saved up a lot of money together, she then took that money and ran away with Ace. Kamal is still hurt that Ace did that to him."

"Wow, everything that girl touches turns to shit." Sammy concluded.

"I'm just happy you are outta jail!" Rhonda speaks with tears of joy in her eyes.

"I'm Brooklyn. It's gonna take more than 72 days of lock down to stop me!"

"Shit if I had 72 days in lock up, they would have to fight to get me out of there!" Marc expresses his delight in being a homosexual male surrounded by other men.

"How is Chyenne and Tay?" Brooklyn questions as she notices that those Sistahs' are not in attendance.

"Crystal dropped all charges against Chyenne about a week ago. We haven't seen her since. You know Chyenne always running from herself." Sammy reports.

"Tay is healing physically but mentally I think she'll be scared forever. She's still in the intensive burn care unit. She is having her 3rd skin surgery tomorrow." Rhonda delivered the news with sorrow in her voice.

"How's my baby Harlem?" Brooklyn questions Sammy.

"Lewis was trying to pull a move but I stopped him in his tracks."

"I bet money that was all his snowflake's idea!" Brooklyn is referring to Lisa, Lewis's wife.

"Calm down Brooklyn! Don't do nothing crazy, you just got out!"

Just as Brooklyn's blood started to boil Dino entered the diner with Harlem in his arms. Dino is now a twenty six year old college student at NYU. He is majoring in Dentistry. Harlem jumped down from Dino's holding arms and ran to Brooklyn's awaiting arms of love. Harlem's little pale arms covered in tiny red freckles wrapped around Brooklyn's neck. Harlem's tiny 4 year old lips planted kisses all up and down Brooklyn's face.

"Luv u, Ma ma. Neva eva lee me again, pinky swear!" Harlem's baby gibberish is music to Brooklyn's ears.

Brooklyn stared into the poetic gray colored eyes shinning bright like Harlem's lights, this is the sight and reason Brooklyn lived. For thirteen years after Carlito, Brooklyn used her beauty to have sex with men to leave them with the vulnerable look in their eyes. She would say it was because she just didn't want a relationship after Carlito but it was because her heart couldn't risk someone turning on her again. When Harlem entered Brooklyn's life, Brooklyn finally received unconditional love. Brooklyn stood up and greeted Dino with a warm embrace.

"Sorry Ma' I tried everything to get Lewis to bend the rules but it's his weekend and he wants Harlem back." Dino delivered the bad news as he waited for the explosion.

"I'll deal with Lewis!" Brooklyn took her attention off Lewis and showered Harlem with her love.

Brooklyn finished talking with the Sistahs'. She showered Harlem with conversation. Dino hated to but he had to break up the reunion between Brooklyn and Harlem to drop her off to her court appointed weekend visits with her father. Rhonda had to run off to King, her fiancé, who was recovering from a serious back injury. Sammy had some appeals to file for one of her custody case. Brooklyn had three hours to kill before she could surprise Le'Roy.

***

Seeing Tay's lifeless body bought Brooklyn's eyes to tears. Tay's mummified body is stiff as a board. She is banged from head to toe. Poor little thing been through 6 skin surgeries. This was the last hope. Tay is suffering from third degree burns inflicted on her by Roc's hand bearing hot water a burn for a burn. He claims Tay gave him HIV. His revenage was the sizzling hot water that peeled her skin off. Mildred has been here by Tay's side since the assault. Mildred is Tay's one of two blood sisters. Mildred was pleading with the lord. Brooklyn sat alongside Tay's hospital bed and prayed. Brooklyn felt like she was looking down onto herself when she was lying in a hospital bed with no hope for living. Brooklyn couldn't stay long; seeing Tay like this was breaking her down.

***

Brooklyn stopped by the *pink pussy cat* to get lingerie that she had bought and left there. She wanted tonight with Le'Roy to be extra sexy and extra special. She didn't expect to find what she did. She heard movement coming from the bathroom. At this very moment Brooklyn was glad she stopped to buy herself a new taser because the police confiscated her old one.

"Hello?" Brooklyn shouts into the apartment with her taser in her hand

"It's just me don't shoot!" Chyenne jokes as she emerges from the bathroom with her hands in the air.

Brooklyn and Chyenne sit and talk. It was like they were teenagers again and Chyenne was pregnant by Ace with Polo. Now Chyenne's belly was filled with Malik's baby. The Sistahs' are 50/50 on the paternity of

Chyenne's unborn baby being that she was openly running around with Ace in Malik's face. Chyenne had decided to run down south to her mother; seeing Malik was currently playing house with Traci was too much for her eyes to take. Chyenne realized that choosing Ace over Malik was the wrong move. She wished her heart would've listened to the Sistahs'. Chyenne wondered did Malik still have something for her. Brooklyn came up with a brilliant idea. Brooklyn had some fake blood in capsules she got from Le'Roy's job. Le'Roy is an electrician at a television station. Brooklyn bust the capsules between Chyenne's legs and called Malik with instructions to meet Chyenne at the hospital. Brooklyn told Chyenne when Malik arrives at the hospital, Brooklyn instructed her to look him in his eyes, the eyes are windows to the heart. Chyenne will know just how Malik feels just from one look. Brooklyn drove Chyenne to the hospital and headed home. Chyenne promised to call Brooklyn with the details of their trickery. Brooklyn opened Le'Roy's apartment door with the spare key he had given to her. She showered and dressed in the red lingerie she picked up for the pink pussy cat. Brooklyn was waiting for Le'Roy when he got home from work. His happiness of seeing Brooklyn was shown in a long hug and passionate kiss. The doors are locked, phones are turned off and windows shut and they opened their minds. Brooklyn had set the pace of freed minds. Their minds traveled miles, driving on sexual appetite. With their minds out of town, their bodies can't be found. All alone, surrounded by four walls. The room was filled with furniture that they tripped over. The thick air of bottled passion clouded their vision. Although they were moving fast they were taking their time to make sure they did it right. He cut to the chase. He grabs her hand and pulls her in to him. He is squeezing her tight as she holds him close to her body. He exhales passion as she inhales his desire. Freeing their skin from clothes and covered their flesh in lust; his lips plant kisses from her head to her toes, special attention to the skin that needs it the most. The growth of longing in her pores guides his touch. His hands are ready to give her what she wants and what she needs. They did whatever turns them on until the stars turn off making dark fantasies become bright reality. Brooklyn was flipped back to front and turned inside out. Acclamation of orgasmic pleasure put Brooklyn to sleep.

"Unfinished business, So whatcha saying?"

"Mandatory" brunch *with E.P.M.D.* E.P.M.D are quadruplets of Carlito's timeless skin. They all are young men but have facial features of teenagers. Brooklyn takes the available seat next to her youngest son, Dino, on his left side. Edwin's serious tensed outlook on life was in his eyes. The stare he inherited from Carlito. For years Brooklyn would avoid eye contact with Edwin to weave Carlito's stares. But today Brooklyn sat across from Edwin staring at him eye to eye. No emotion could be read from Edwin's expression. Pedro sat next to Edwin. Pedro tapped his cigarette lighter on the diner's table. Miguel is the computer genius. He is working on a computer program on his laptop at the diner's table.

"Le dan la bienvenida[53]" Edwin sling the words in Brooklyn's face.

"For what?" Brooklyn questions.

"For paying Marquez to get you outta jail!" Edwin's words of information was delivered with Carlito's eyes.

"OH, really! I hope you spent ya own money? Why would you help her? She killed Papi and left Abuela to be buried in American soil, against her dying wish. I'm sick of this shit! Why can't y'all see her for what she is?" Pedro's words that was thrown in the air are filled with his hot temper.

---

[53] *Le dan la bienvenida* translates to *"You welcome."*

Pedro slammed his fist down on the table. Normally Pedro's outburst would make Brooklyn cringe but she didn't bat an eye.

"Pedro, if you have something to say to me say it to me! I'm sitting right here!" Brooklyn spoke with her hand in her purse. Brooklyn had her finger on the trigger of her taser.

"Stupid!" Pedro slaps Edwin in the back of his head with his hand and words.

"No matter what she did or didn't do she is still our mother."

"Malvavisco![54] just say you love her and forget about what she did to Papi"

---

[54] **Malvavisco** *translates to marshmallow*

Pedro shouts as he hits the table again.

"Pedro, I'm gonna have to ask you to respect my mother in my presence." Dino delivered his words strong and solid.

"Thank you Edwin, I appreciate what you did for me." Brooklyn voices her gratitude.

"You welcome Ma', I would like to introduce you to my family, will you meet them?"

"Sure son, will you be willing to meet your sister Harlem?"

"I met her already Dino brought her by the house. She's beautiful."

"Well let's just start singing kumbaya! Fuck this I'll never trust her, ***ella está maldita!***[55]" Pedro words was thrown over his shoulder as he exits the diner.

Pedro has the temper of Carlito. His tactic of playing on Brooklyn's fear is to break, hit and punch things to let out his hot temper. He has broken many of Brooklyn's indian artifacts that she collects, indulging in the illusion of her appearance. Carlito use to break, hit and punch on Brooklyn to let out his frustrations. Miguel is still the quiet one. One could forget he was in the room, he never talked. He has the knowledge of speaking but only exercised the right when it was necessary.

---

[55] ***Ella está maldita*** *translates to "She's cursed."*

"He is high Ma, don't take it personal." Miguel words calmed Brooklyn's disappointment in Pedro.

Brooklyn sat and had brunch with her three sons. It was like she was meeting these fine young men for the first time. For the first time Brooklyn looked at her sons faces and saw them not Carlito in them. Brooklyn was hurting that Pedro didn't stand by her like she had for him. Pedro had disturbed people's property, shoplifted and tortured the neighbor's pets. Brooklyn knew Pedro was guilty of the 15 missing cats in the neighborhood but argued anybody down that accused him.

***

"New beginnings?" Lewis questions.

"Yes, new beginnings. I realized fighting with you ain't really worth it. We can share Harlem, with boundaries."

"I've talked to Vanessa. I sincerely doubt she'll be saying anything to you. She is afraid for her life. She over heard in the nail salon you killed Carlito."

"And what do you think?"

"I think you are more than capable of killing anyone especially Carlito. Surprisingly my answer is NO I don't think you killed him."

"Thank you Lewis. So we agree you will take care of Vanessa while we take care of Harlem?"

"Agreed!"

***

"To be 100 percent true to myself I must tell Le'Roy who I really am. I believe everything I've experienced makes me who I am today. I really like him but he is looking for love and I will never be able to open my heart to a man. I just couldn't risk having a locked heart again. Our short time together was amazing but I can't intentionally hurt him I gotta let him go."

"Slumber to the bruises and the sores, awake my life"

Brooklyn is standing over Carlito's grave with EPMD. She promised the boys to attend the memorial visit. Pedro's weeps like it was a funeral service, when Carlito has been dead for a year.

"For a long time I held rage in my heart for you and everything you did to me. I'm no longer angry. You are where you belong."

"Did you know him?" the younger woman questions Brooklyn.

Brooklyn eyeballs the young woman. The young woman has a familiar face.

"Yes, unfortunately" Brooklyn answers still glaring at the young woman.

Brooklyn was trying to give a name to the face but nothing was coming to mind.

"Who are you?" Brooklyn mouth speaks the words of her mind.

"I'm his daughter, I watched him beat my mother. He broke her ribs. The broken rib punctured her lungs. We had a donor and he refused to give us a single penny. So I shot his ass and took the money. I ran to the hospital with the bloody money in my hand but I was 3 minutes too late... my mother had just died." The young woman spat on Carlito's grave before she walked away with anger in her heart.

EPMD's eyes had locked with Brooklyn's eyes. Pedro weeped harder. The shame of how he had treated his mother was eating him up inside. Brooklyn stood stiff as a board as her eyes stared in to space. She had just met Carlito's killer and Mercedes's daughter.

"I'm sorry to say I didn't feel anything for Mercedes. What did she think was going to happen? Did she think Carlito was able to love any one besides himself? I'm happy the young girl took Carlito out his misery but I was furious she had stolen the opportunity from me. I wanted to have Carlito on his knees begging for his life as somebody ran up in his cheeks." Brooklyn's chitachatter.

EPMD surrounds Brooklyn and wrap their arms around her. In that very moment the memories came to life and they remembered Carlito for the father he was and not the father they wanted him to be. They also remembered Brooklyn as their mother and not the words of Brooklyn planted in their minds by Carlito. They loved their mother and in this very moment they promised to never abandon their mother the way she had been before for so long. They were filled with apologies. As Brooklyn and EPMD began to walk away from Carlito's dark grave and toward a bright future a man blocked their path. Brooklyn thought her eyes were playing tricks on her but she was face to face with her treat of memory.

"I came for you, like I promised! I'm ready now and so are you. It took us both years to clean up our past. Will you spend the rest of your life with me? Now that we can start from today with the people we are today" Hugo questions Brooklyn with a ring box.

A tear-filled "YES" was all Brooklyn could say.

"When spring is in the air, love is near."

"You have to breathe. When you get another contraction let me know okay?"

"OHHHHHHHH HERE'S ANOTHER ONE!" Chyenne shouts.

Malik is staring down on Chyenne's forehead. Malik is mesmerized by her beauty glowing under the sweat beads rolling down her face. Malik's mind remembers the woman he fell in love with, while his eyes see the woman that betrayed him for a childhood first love. As Chyenne grips Malik's hands. She is holding on to past, when this man was her husband and not the man that cheated on her. At the present moment she saw Malik before his cheating actions resulted in a baby girl.

Malik rubs the back of her hand. He didn't remember how smooth her skin was until now.

"PUSH PUSH! Great job! One more and it all be over!"

"I'M READY!"

Malik eyes are filled with tears of love and emotion. When the doctor handed Malik his son, Malik tears streamed down his cheek. Malik vowed to never leave "their" side.

To be continued.....

Chitter Chatter 2

For information or to get help, please call:

The National Domestic Violence Hotline:

1*800*799*7233

The National Sexual Assault Hotline:

1*800*656*4673

The National Teen Dating Abuse Hotline:

1*866*331*9474